What was it about Sarah that was different from all the others?

She brought out a surge of protectiveness and tenderness, true. He wanted to hold her, protect her. But why? Why her? His feelings were disconcerting.

Justin shook his head, feeling an emotion churning in his gut.

Loneliness.

He had to admit he was lonely. He loved his daughter. But he missed having someone closer around to share his experiences with. Someone to talk with in the evening when he got home from work, someone to laugh with over a joke or share those little secret smiles when Mickie did something really adorable. Someone to hold when he felt overwhelmed. Someone to love with all his heart.

But Sarah?

No. *Anyone* but her....

Books by Cheryl Wolverton

Love Inspired

A Matter of Trust #11
A Father's Love #20
This Side of Paradise #38
The Best Christmas Ever #47
A Mother's Love #63
For Love of Zach #76
For Love of Hawk #87
What the Doctor Ordered #99
For Love of Mitch #105

Healing Hearts #118
A Husband To Hold #136
In Search of a Hero #166
†*A Wife for Ben* #192
†*Shelter from the Storm* #198
Once Upon a Chocolate Kiss #229
Among the Tulips #257
Home to You #332

Love Inspired Suspense

†*Storm Clouds* #7

*Hill Creek, Texas
†Everyday Heroes

CHERYL WOLVERTON

RITA® Award finalist Cheryl Wolverton has well over a dozen books to her name. Her very popular HILL CREEK, TEXAS series has been a finalist in many contests. Having grown up in Oklahoma, lived in Kentucky, Texas, Louisiana and now living once more in Oklahoma, Cheryl and her husband of more than twenty years and their two children, Jeremiah and Christina, always considered themselves Oklahomans transplanted to grow and flourish in the South. Readers are always welcome to contact her via mail, P.O. Box 106, Faxon, OK 73540 or e-mail at Cheryl@cherylwolverton.com. You can also visit her Web site at www.cherylwolverton.com.

The Best
Christmas Ever
Cheryl Wolverton

Steeple
Hill®

Published by Steeple Hill Books™

STEEPLE HILL BOOKS

Steeple
Hill®

ISBN-13: 978-0-373-36087-1
ISBN-10:   0-373-36087-8

THE BEST CHRISTMAS EVER

This edition published by arrangement with Steeple Hill Books.

® and TM are trademarks of Steeple Hill Books, used under license. Trademarks indicated with ® are registered in the United States Patent and Trademark Office, the Canadian Trade Marks Office and in other countries.

www.SteepleHill.com

Printed in U.S.A.

For the Lord loves the just and will not forsake
His faithful ones.
They will be protected forever....
—*Psalms* 37:28

To Janet Abbott for always listening.
Thanks to Anne Canadeo, the greatest editor
in the world, and Jean Price, the greatest agent!
And I can't forget Dee Pace—
who went above and beyond for this book!
Thanks! And three other very special ladies:
Denise Gray, Donna Blacklock and Cheryl Crews.

With love to my husband who is so patient and
thoughtful when I'm going crazy over computer
problems, and my kids, Christina and Jeremiah.
You guys are the love of my life.

Prologue

Dear Santa:

All I want this year for Christmas is a mommy. I know it's sorta early still to ask, but it is almost cold out, and I miss Mommy, and so does Daddy. He doesn't exactly say he misses her, but he stares at Mommy's picture a lot. I heard my baby-sitter on the phone telling someone Daddy needed to get married again. Well, that'd mean I'd get a new mommy. And if I had a new mommy, then I wouldn't have to play Go Fish with Daddy's secretary anymore when he couldn't find a baby-sitter. And I wouldn't have to take store-bought cookies on party day at school. I could have a real mommy to bake chocolate chip cookies—and make me peanut butter-and-jelly sandwiches as much as I wanted. But most of all, Santa, I would have a mommy to hug me the way the other kids do when we get out of school. It would be just too cool to have that. So, Santa, that's what I've decided I want for Christmas. I told Jesus so He can look around for the right mommy, then tell you which one to bring me on Christmas Eve. I know this is going to be the best Christmas present ever.

Thank you, Santa.

Signed,
Mickie Warner

Chapter One

"Sarah?"

Sarah Connelly smiled sweetly at her brother-in-law's incredulous tone, then watched as his surprise slowly turned to cool remoteness. "Surely, Justin, it hasn't been so long that you've forgotten me," she quipped, doing her best to hide her fear that he'd slam the door in her face.

His mask fell into place just the way Sarah remembered it had in the past. His critical gaze slowly took her in. Sarah did her best not to gather the thin sweater around her shoulders against the cold wind or his icy scrutiny.

"Maybe it's just because I've never seen you in jeans," he replied indifferently. "Remember the last time I saw you—in court? That nice little blue suit you wore when…"

"Yes, well." Sarah shrugged dismissively.

"So what brings you here?" He leaned against the

door frame, blocking her way into his house. "It has, after all, been two years."

"I wanted to see Mickie," she replied, deciding that any hope she'd had of getting the baby-sitting/housekeeper job was just a dream. He was still furious with her, and she didn't blame him. Although she'd hoped it would be different.

"I don't think that's a good idea."

"I'm her aunt."

"Who hasn't been here in two years," he retorted.

"I'm sorry." Sarah shifted her chilled feet, pushing at the loose strand of blond hair that blew across her face. She was cold. Justin knew she was cold, but he wasn't going to let her in.

"Sorry?" Justin's eyes flashed. "For what? For not coming to see Mickie? Or for trying to take her away from me two years ago?"

Instead of getting angry as she would have back then, Sarah dropped her gaze from Justin's accusing one. "Both," she finally whispered. Lifting her chin, she forced a smile. "Look, I wanted to apologize and put it all behind us, but I guess that's impossible. I'll be going."

All she wanted to do was leave. She'd known it was a stupid idea to come here and apply for the job. But her friend Bill had been so certain Justin would take her on. Of course, Bill was newly married and in love. He thought all families loved one another the way he loved his in-laws. He couldn't understand the icy wall of anger and bitterness that separated her and Justin, the guilt and fears....

Justin's hand shot out and wrapped around her small arm. "Wait."

She froze at Justin's first touch, then slowly turned. Indecision and frustration etched his rugged features. He wasn't sure if he wanted her there or not. The years hadn't changed him. Justin was still as good-looking as when she'd first met him almost seven years ago. A few gray hairs she didn't remember were now mixed in his dark brown wavy hair. It was cut short in the back and longer on the top; one lock of his hair fell casually out of place over his forehead. He hadn't gained an ounce of weight. "Since when do you wear jeans?" She liked the way he looked in them.

He cocked an eyebrow in amusement.

Warmth climbed her face as she realized she'd actually asked the question out loud.

"Since I've been doing the housework," he replied evenly.

She fidgeted a moment, then stepped back. "Well, I'd better go—"

"No. I..." He ran a hand through his hair, his other hand on his hip. Finally, he sighed. "It's been two years, Sarah. Why now?"

"You already asked that," Sarah replied with the only comeback she could think of that would give her time to form an answer.

"Daddy?"

Justin's head jerked toward the stairs.

Sarah saw panic in his eyes. "Look, Justin, if you don't want Mickie to see me I'll go. I understand if—"

"No, come on in." A long, low breath escaped Justin before he stepped back to allow her in.

Turning toward the stairs, he called up, "I'll be right there, Mickie. Go ahead and put on the jeans I laid out for you."

He stepped back and allowed Sarah to enter the house. It hadn't changed since her sister, Amy, had lived there two years ago. The same overstuffed sofa filled the living room; an oak coffee table still sat in front of the sofa, with a book of scenic landscapes throughout America on it. On the mantel framed family photos were arranged with pride and loving care. Looking out through the open curtains, Sarah saw the sky was still clouded over and it looked as though it might rain or snow any moment.

"Mickie has been asking about relatives lately. I suppose it wouldn't hurt to let you meet with her. Just don't do anything to hurt her."

Sarah jerked as if she'd been slapped. "I'd never hurt Mickie."

"Then why'd you try to take her away from me two years ago?"

This was the question Sarah had not wanted to hear. The accusation and suppressed anger in his voice were as obvious as the fact that he expected her to answer. "I truly thought she'd be better off with me, Justin," she finally said.

He snorted. "I'm sure your fiancé would love having her with you now, wouldn't he, Sarah?"

Sarah stiffened. "How do you know about André?"

"Hamilton is a small town," he replied, shrugging. Of course everyone in the small suburb well outside the Dallas-Fort Worth metropolis knew everything about everyone. She paled, wondering if he knew the rest, too. She didn't dare ask. Instead, she said, "André likes children."

That much was true.

"So, do you still work as your fiancé's secretary?"

"So, do you still take people's business away from them?" she retorted, and was immediately contrite at the look of pain that flashed in Justin's eyes. "I'm sorry. I didn't mean that." She placed her hands on her hips, her exasperation evident in every inch of her stiff body. "Why must you be so provoking, Justin? I came here to apologize, to put the past in the past. We're family. Mickie is the only blood relative I have left. I want to get to know her. I thought you might be able to forgive me for that reason alone."

It had taken two years. She'd had to hit rock bottom and turn to God before realizing how much she'd wronged this man. But once she had acknowledged what a grievous blow she'd dealt Justin by taking him to court for custody of Mickie, she'd hoped to correct it. Her only mistake was in listening to Bill and deciding to apply for the job as housekeeper.

Of course, now that she saw how Justin still felt about her, she couldn't tell him about what she'd found out from the doctor. Or how that had led to André breaking off their engagement. Nor how that had led to the sweet note in her mailbox the following week saying that Watson and Watson had to cut back staff and she, unfortunately, was the one who had to go.

André hadn't even had the guts to fire her in person.

That still hurt. But she knew God had a reason for all that happened. She knew now that if she trusted Him, He would turn everything out for the good. It was His way even when she couldn't see it herself.

Justin sighed again. "You're right. I'm sorry, too."

"I really do want to try to get along."

Justin ran a hand through his hair.

"For Amy's sake," she said, then added more desperately, "for Mickie's sake."

That swayed him. "You're right. Despite how angry I am at you, Mickie needs to know you. Other kids at kindergarten have been asking about her family. The kids at school all have aunts and uncles."

She heard the silent *and a mother.*

"I think she'd really like to meet a relative. But if you hurt her or say anything—"

"I won't," Sarah cut in. Since her devastating news and resulting breakup with André she'd had a lot of time to think and pray.

She wanted to know Mickie. She'd allowed two years to pass since the court battle, and hadn't seen Mickie since. It was time to forget the past and go forward. And she wanted to do that with the only family she had left.

"Look, I have an important meeting I'll be late for if I don't get ready. I'll go up and change. I'll tell Mickie you're here."

"Will she know who I am?"

Justin scowled. "She knows she has an aunt Sarah. You can visit with her until the baby-sitter gets here. If all goes well, then we'll see about visits after that.

I'd better warn you, though—Mickie doesn't take well to strangers, whether she's heard of them or not.''

Sarah nodded.

Without another word, Justin turned and headed up the stairs.

The kids at school all have aunts and uncles.

Sarah's heart ached at his words. How much had Mickie missed because of her mother's death, because of Sarah's bitterness and anger, because of the bitterness and anger between her and Justin?

Well, she was going to set things right if she could, starting now.

A sound at the top of the stairs caught her attention and she looked up. A five-year-old girl, with long brown curly hair that hung past her shoulders stood at the top of the stairs, a fashion doll clutched in her hands.

The child studied Sarah a long minute before slowly descending. ''Daddy says you're my aunt.''

Tears welled in Sarah's eyes, but she quickly blinked them away. Mickie looked so much like Amy it hurt to see her. She wanted to grab the child and hug her, never let her go, but she knew Mickie didn't remember her. ''That's right, Michelle,'' she said, trying to hide her trembling by clasping her hands.

''Daddy calls me 'Mickie.''

Of course, Sarah thought, not even knowing why she had used the child's given name. ''That's right. Your mom said that was the first word out of your daddy's mouth when you were born.''

Mickie's eyes widened. ''Did you know my mama?''

"Yes, sweetheart, I did. Your mama was my sister."

Mickie's wide brown eyes, the only thing she had inherited from her father, stared at Sarah as if assessing that bit of information.

"Her picture looks like you. Will you tell me her favorite story?"

Sarah reached out for the child's hand. After Mickie slipped her tiny one into hers, she led her over to the couch. "Of course I will," she said, humbled that Mickie took her in without questioning why she'd never come by or why she'd missed birthdays and Christmases. "Her favorite story was *The Littlest Angel*. Have you ever heard that?"

Mickie shook her head and Sarah settled her in to tell her the tale.

Upstairs, Justin listened to the murmuring below. He'd told Sarah Mickie didn't usually take to people, but Mickie had been so excited when she'd found out her aunt Sarah had come to visit. Knowing the sitter would be there any minute, he'd allowed Mickie to go down by herself.

It was the least he could do after telling Sarah never to come near his child again. Sarah had attempted to breach the wall between them. He wouldn't reinforce the barricade by refusing to trust her for a few minutes with his daughter. After all, what could happen?

The ringing phone interrupted his thoughts. Pulling on his long-sleeved white shirt, he crossed the room to answer it. "Hello?"

It was Mrs. Winters, the baby-sitter. "Justin. I know I was supposed to baby-sit tonight, but I just got a call fifteen minutes ago from my daughter out in Arizona. She's gone into early labor and it's not going well. I've had to book an emergency flight and am leaving within the hour. Justin?''

Barely able to restrain a groan of dismay, he replied, ''I understand, Mrs. Winters. I'll be praying for your daughter.''

''I really hate to do this. I know I told you I'd be able to work at least three more weeks, but pregnancies just aren't always predictable.''

''Don't worry,'' he said, even as he silently went through a list, trying to figure out whom he could round up to watch his daughter on such a short notice. ''I'll find someone. You just worry about getting to your daughter's side. I'll be fine.''

Justin could hear the relief in Mrs. Winters's voice as she hung up the phone. It might be relief for her, but it was near chaos for him. He had to make that important business meeting scheduled in less than an hour with the top executives of a software firm on the West Coast. His second-in-command, Phillip, had worked out most of the negotiations over the phone. This was the only time the executives could meet with Justin to sign the papers and go over last-minute details before the merger was completed.

Why did things have to get so messed up now? If he called off the meeting, the men might lose confidence in him and go to another company. They were desperate and needed this...and so did he. His company had suffered financial setbacks the past few years, but he had finally turned things around. With this merger, his firm would again be one of the biggest producers of software components in the southwestern United States.

He finished buttoning his shirt, then grabbed his tie and draped it around his neck. After picking up his jacket, he headed downstairs. Justin supposed he could take Mickie with him to the meeting. He'd set her up someplace comfortable with books and toys and hope she'd manage to amuse herself. He'd done it before. But this meeting would last longer than most, and be more delicate. Maybe he could call Phillip, who had picked up the businessmen from the airport, and have him stall....

Coming down the stairs, he was surprised when he saw Sarah on his couch. He had forgotten she was there.

Finally continuing on, he reached the bottom of the stairs before she spotted him and her murmurs to Mickie drifted off. Justin tossed his jacket on the back of the sofa and worked his tie into an acceptable knot. "Mickie, I need you to go upstairs and change. That was Mrs. Winters on the phone and she can't baby-sit tonight. You'll have to come with me to work." Seeing her downcast look, he decided to remind her of his secretary's presence. "Christine will be there and maybe she can play with you while I work. You love to play with her." It wasn't exactly true and he was feeling guilty for suggesting it. Mickie tolerated the older woman's game of Go Fish and her comments about her pretty little dresses.

"What about Aunt Sarah?"

Justin's gaze shifted to Sarah. He still couldn't believe he'd almost forgotten she was there. That was very odd. In the past, every time they'd been in the same room a yelling match had ensued within minutes of their arrivals and she'd stormed off in a huff. Why was she being so quiet today? Her deep blue eyes blinked and he could have sworn she was embarrassed to be caught in the family emergency. Hah! Unlikely. Sarah loved controversy.

"What about her?"

"Why can't she watch me?"

"Mickie," her father warned, surprised by his daughter's unusual show of spirit.

"I don't think your daddy would like that." Realizing what she'd said, Sarah gazed at her brother-in-law in shocked apology.

Justin didn't know what to say. He wanted to tell her, *Impossible, there's no way I'd trust my daughter with you. You despise me.* But then he couldn't get over her look of embarrassment at what she'd just said. No matter how true it was that he and Sarah didn't get along, he didn't want his daughter to know that, which made him realize just how wrong his feelings were. But it would take time to get over those feelings.

Do unto others...

The verse he'd learned as a child floated into his mind, striking him with guilt. What was he teaching his daughter by harboring this anger? And what would she think if he didn't at least try to work through his pain and forgive his sister-in-law? It was true Mickie might not understand everything that had happened, but she would understand her aunt Sarah not coming around again.

Justin finally said, albeit reluctantly, "Actually, Sarah, if you're available for the rest of the evening, I wouldn't mind. Mickie seems quite taken by her aunt. And it'd give you a little more time to visit."

Sarah swallowed her automatic no. She knew Justin didn't really want her there. But could she have ever, in her wildest dreams, envisioned spending an evening with her niece? She hadn't seen Mickie since her sister's funeral. Mickie had not been at the hearing before the judge. Sarah hadn't been dismayed over that. She had believed she'd have Mickie soon enough.

How absolutely arrogant she had been, and how angry when the court had ruled in her brother-in-law's favor. Now she was getting a second chance to know Mickie, to get reacquainted with her. The door had just been opened; the opportunity she had been praying for had dropped into her lap. "I don't have to be anywhere. I'd be glad to watch her."

An awkward silence fell as the two adults stared at each other; it was broken finally when Mickie squealed in glee and clapped her hands.

"Will you fix me dinner? I like fried chicken, but Daddy doesn't make it. I also like peanut butter-and-jelly sandwiches. And then you can help me into my 'jamas and we can read stories till Dad gets home. Is that okay, Daddy? Can we read stories until you get home?"

Sarah saw Justin's features soften and was amazed at how much younger he looked when he smiled so gently like that. "That sounds fine."

When his gaze returned to Sarah, the cool mask fell back in place.

"There's a list of emergency numbers by the phone. Fix whatever you two decide you want for dinner...except peanut butter-and-jelly sandwiches." He cast a warning look at his daughter, who bowed her head and appeared properly contrite at the idea of allowing any peanut butter or jelly to pass her lips again in the near future. "I should be home sometime this evening. The office is about forty-five minutes away and the people I'm meeting have to leave tonight."

He looked at his watch. Four o'clock. He would be late at this rate. Thank goodness he had arranged to meet them at a hotel closer to his home. It had been Phillip's idea to pick them up in the limo and for them all to go to the office together for the tour and business meeting. "Any questions?"

Sarah shook her head. Still he seemed unsure. "Look, Justin," she said, "if you want, I'll call you every hour on the hour. You don't need to worry that we'll be gone when you return." She didn't tell him that she no longer had a car and had caught the bus over. Call it pride, but she just couldn't admit that.

His face didn't show if that was what he was thinking or not. He finally sighed and gave a curt nod. "I'm trusting you on this. My secretary's number is on the list. Phone if you need anything."

He kissed his daughter goodbye and headed out the door.

Sarah couldn't believe it. She was actually alone with her niece. Why had Justin allowed it?

Was it that it had been so long and he'd relegated the past to the past? She wondered if he meant to pay her. There was no way she would ask. She wasn't even sure she could take his money. She was desperate, but was she that desperate?

True, that was why she'd originally come. But she hadn't expected to feel guilty and uncomfortable around Justin. Had she thought to be that same old arrogant woman who would look at him as though he owed her for his past sins?

Closing her mind to those questions, she turned her attention to Mickie, who was tugging on her shirt.

"Can we cook now? I like to help in the kitchen, but Mrs. Winters never lets me. She says I make a mess, especially when we have chicken. You know, we wouldn't have to have peanut butter-and-jelly *sandwiches*. Sometimes Daddy lets me eat them on crackers, too."

Sarah smiled. She hadn't eaten since last night. She'd missed breakfast this morning because she had wanted to find somewhere to shower before coming over to Justin's. The only other meal she'd have a chance at was dinner at six o'clock in the evening.

Oh, no! She suddenly focused on one small fact she'd conveniently forgotten; she had to be back by eight o'clock. Would Justin be home before then? She worried her bottom lip, then sighed. Well, there was no choice now. She'd just have to hope it worked out.

"I think peanut butter and jelly on anything is out—if that look your father gave you was any indication," she said, forcing her worries from her mind. She'd have plenty of time later to worry. Right now she wanted to soak up Mickie's presence. "Come on, let's go thaw out something and you can help me make a mess in the kitchen."

"You make a mess?"

Mickie's eyes widened in childish horror. Sarah smiled. "It's more fun that way." She winked.

Going toward the kitchen with Mickie, Sarah realized that things might actually be changing in her life. Maybe the past could be just that—the past. Maybe she could forget it; let go of the ghosts that haunted her, the mistakes she had made. Perhaps she could turn over a new leaf and start back on the right path. It'd been so long…she wasn't sure if she could even find her way back on her own. How did she get rid of years of bitterness and pain and find peace again with the very person she had wronged?

She remembered then—something her mother had told her when she'd had a fight with her dear friend and they had stopped talking for two weeks. She'd been frantic that she would never see her friend again and didn't know if Sylvia would accept her apology or not. She'd prayed but wasn't sure God had answered her prayer on how she should ask forgiveness for yelling at Sylvia.

"When you turn and walk down our street it takes five minutes to reach the end, dear. How long does it take to return?"

She had answered, "Five minutes."

"And how do you get back? Do you cover that distance in five seconds or fifty seconds? Do you turn and take different streets to get you back to our house?"

"No, Mama," she'd replied.

"That's right, dear. You simply turn around and start from the way you came, taking one step at a time.

Sometimes you can make it a little faster, sometimes not. But the important thing is you make that decision and turn around and go back.''

Her mother had been right. By confronting the issue with Sylvia, Sarah had righted things, although the lost trust between them had taken a little longer to return.

Now she knew that no matter how long it took, she wanted things right again between her and her only living relative. So maybe, if she prayed—since the first step to anything was prayer, or at least that was what she'd been taught in her family—this time things would be different between her and her brother-in-law. They could get along well enough that she would again have a family.

If she hadn't turned her back and run from God when everything had happened almost seven years ago, then this mess wouldn't have happened.

She told herself to remember that this time and everything *would* work out. Put God first, not her own selfish feelings, and trust God to work the miracle.

Looking down at Mickie, she knew that no matter what happened, she had to do that. She didn't want to lose what she only now was discovering filled a void that had long been in need of filling.

Chapter Two

The click of the door told Sarah that Justin had returned. She put down the book she'd been thumbing through and stood. Even in the darkened light of the living room Justin looked good. Tired, but good. His suit jacket was thrown over his shoulder and a hint of beard shadowed his square jaw. Dark brown eyes scanned the room before landing on her.

"Mickie asleep?"

Sarah unclasped her hands. "Yes. She fell asleep about an hour ago."

Silence fell and Sarah resisted the urge to shift. It was late and for the past hour she'd been wondering how to handle Justin's reappearance. Before, Mickie had been a buffer between them. Now that buffer was gone and she wasn't sure how to act or how her brother-in-law would act. She cleared her throat. "Well, I'd better go."

She started toward the door.

When her hand was on the knob, Justin spoke. "What really brought you here, Sarah?"

She stiffened. How could she tell him that in desperation she'd come to him for a job? He wouldn't believe it. Or worse. He might. And then he'd either laugh at her or pity her. He certainly wouldn't hire her, knowing she had been let go from her job in a lawyer's office, no matter what the reason. Doubts and fears crushed in on her, making her shoulders heavy with the burden of carrying them. Sarah forced herself to stand up straight, as if Justin might actually see the weight loading her down. "I came to bury the hatchet," she quipped, without turning around to face him.

A wry chuckle escaped Justin's lips and Sarah felt a warm tingle run down her back. Had that laugh attracted Amy? She knew it certainly affected her.

"Well then," he said when silence had fallen again, "maybe I should be glad you didn't decide to bury it in my neck like…"

She knew what he would have said—*Like when you tried to take Mickie.* She stiffened. "Good night."

"Wait." Justin rested his hand on her shoulder even as she pulled open the door. "I'm sorry."

She didn't respond but stood facing the door, hiding her eyes from his scrutiny lest he see what she was feeling.

"Will it always be this way between us?" he finally asked.

"I don't know," Sarah replied.

With a sigh, he released her.

Sarah walked out the door, deciding that she was

walking out of his life for the final time. Turning down the street, she headed to where she hoped she'd be able to catch the last bus for the night, wondering why she'd ever thought she could work for the man her sister had married.

Justin leaned his head against the closed door and sighed again. He was tired. The meeting had been a lot more complicated than he'd expected. What was supposed to be a simple merger had turned into more negotiations. Years ago he wouldn't have allowed it, but because he'd seen these men making a sincere effort to protect their employees, he'd spent the extra two hours negotiating. Then they'd had to have a new contract typed and finally signed. The men had fortunately found seats on a later flight. It was almost eleven o'clock and he'd been worried about his daughter…and he'd treated Sarah badly.

Pushing away from the door, he turned, then went through the house, flipping off lights and checking windows. There had been no reason for him to say such cruel things to her. Indeed, she'd been trying to bury the hatchet. That was the longest they'd gone without snipping at each other. And then he'd had to ruin it. She was Amy's sister—the only link he and Mickie had to Amy. The least he could have done was hold his tongue. It was just that when he'd opened the door and seen her rising from the couch, the book of scenic landscapes sliding from her lap, he'd felt as though someone had punched him in the gut. He'd never noticed that Sarah was a very beautiful woman, despite her beat-up jeans and sweater. He'd always pictured her as tough and aggressive. Her soft golden hair, which she'd always worn up, had floated about her face tonight, giving her the look of innocence wronged. But he'd not wronged her. And she wasn't innocent or soft. He knew her real personality. She had tried to take his daughter away. He'd been right to fight her to keep his child. And he wouldn't forget the pain that fight had caused anytime soon, no matter how innocent or beautiful she looked.

He hadn't felt a spark of interest in a woman since Amy's death. How could that spark be ignited by the sister who had caused them both so much grief? In anger at his own reaction to her, he'd struck out.

He trudged up the stairs. After checking on Mickie to make sure she was covered, he undressed.

Because of his actions, Mickie would probably never see Sarah again. She'd be stuck with a baby-sitter all day—

Baby-sitter!

Justin didn't have a baby-sitter for his daughter, tomorrow or anytime. He collapsed on the side of the bed and dropped his head into his hands. How could he have forgotten?

Easy. Big blue eyes and a heart-stopping smile had clouded his thinking.

Well, he couldn't let them distract him now. He had to find someone for tomorrow. Justin lifted his head. Maybe this was a way to prove to Sarah that he wanted to accept her apology and make amends. He could ask her to baby-sit this weekend, since she probably didn't work on weekends, and Mickie could get to know her. Of course his day would be short on Saturday. He only had to finish up the paperwork related to tonight's merger and make sure everything was running smoothly. Then he could invite Sarah over for dinner on Sunday as a gesture of thanks. That should smooth over the mistake he'd made tonight.

He reached into the drawer by his bed and pulled out the phone book. After finding her number, he dialed it.

He listened as the call connected.

On the third ring, instead of an answering machine picking up, he heard a message saying the phone was disconnected.

Frowning, he put the receiver down. Had she moved lately? He called Information and the operator told him she had no listing under Sarah's name.

Thinking back, he remembered Bill, from church, mentioning he'd talked to Sarah only last week. He hadn't said where he'd seen her or what they'd talked about. His friends were that way. If they met up with Sarah they only informed him that they'd seen her. Few of his friends felt the need to gossip and dredge up past pains. And, he thought, a few were still friends with Sarah, though none ever really talked about her when he was around.

Bill was the answer. If it had been only last week since he'd talked to her he would know where she was now living. Despite the late hour, Justin picked up the phone and dialed Bill's number. On the second ring, Bill answered it. Justin smiled. Bill had a thing for computers and was usually up until one or two in the morning playing around with some new software or game.

"Hey, Bill," he said. "Uh, sorry to call so late."

"Justin? No problem. I'm up. What's going on?"

"I just tried to get hold of Sarah. She stopped by earlier today and I need to talk to her. I tried the phone number I have for her, but the service has been disconnected. I figured you could tell me where she moved."

Silence followed.

Justin frowned.

Finally, Bill spoke, but it wasn't with the answer Justin had wanted.

"You say you talked to her today?"

"Yeah. She, uh, watched Mickie for me. I was in a bind—"

"You let her baby-sit your daughter?"

Why was Bill sounding so shocked? "Yeah. She came by to visit. My baby-sitter had an emergency and Mickie seemed taken with Sarah. Look," Justin said, becoming impatient, "do you know where she moved? I'd like to get hold of her." Suddenly, it dawned on Justin what had been bothering him. Her number had not been changed but disconnected. Why? Wait a minute. She had been engaged— "Or what her new last name is," he added, drawing the conclusion that she must now be married and that was why she no longer had a phone number of her own. "I'd like to…thank her," he finished, thinking that if she was married, then she wouldn't want to baby-sit on a weekend. He couldn't believe she had stayed tonight with a husband waiting for her at home. At least her marriage explained her decreased anger and bitterness since the last time they'd seen each other.

''Sarah didn't tell you?''

Confused, Justin wrinkled his brow. ''Tell me what? That she had married? No, but I know she was engaged—''

''*Was* is the operative word there, buddy. You'd better sit down.''

Justin stood, instead. ''Look, Bill, obviously you know something I don't. Why don't you try telling me.''

''I don't know all the particulars. Just that she's no longer engaged.''

''Is that all?''

''No. As a matter of fact, it's not. She no longer works for her fiancé's family, either, as of a very short time ago. Nor does she live in her old apartment.''

Justin sighed impatiently. ''I know the latter—that's why I called you. Do you know where she lives?''

''Yes.''

Restlessly, Justin ran a hand through his hair. Why was Bill acting as if Sarah's address and phone number were a national secret? Okay, so Bill felt sorry for Sarah. She had broken off with her fiancé and quit her job. Justin was sorry for her, too, but that might just work out to his best. Maybe he could hire Sarah for a week or two until she found a better job...unless she already had one. But first he had to locate her. This was all too much to take in at once. Just what did he really know about Sarah? Very little, he suddenly realized.

''So where is she?'' he demanded, quickly reaching the end of his rope.

There was a hesitation, then a sigh. "Look, Justin, maybe since she didn't tell you—"

"Where, Bill?" he demanded.

"Okay, okay! But if she's mad at me—"

"Bill!"

"She's living at a homeless shelter downtown near Second Street."

Justin's legs collapsed underneath him and he sank to the bed, stunned. "Homeless shelter?" he whispered, unable to believe what he was hearing.

"Yeah. Evidently, when she lost her job, she didn't have enough money to pay her rent. She had to move out but had nowhere to go and wouldn't let me help since I'm so newly married. She refuses to collect unemployment—"

"She was fired!" Justin shouted.

"As I said," Bill continued without answering Justin's question, "she comes in twice a week, looking for a job. The law office, it seems, was overstaffed and had to get rid of a secretary."

"What's the shelter's name and number?"

"Why?"

"Because I'm going to call and leave a message for Sarah to expect me."

"Sorry, bud, the shelter closes its doors at eight. Which also means no phone calls, either."

"What do you mean, it closes its doors at eight?"

"Just what I said. Haven't you ever been around shelters? In the morning the people are fed, then put out for the day. At the end of the day the shelters reopen and the occupants are allowed back in for supper. At eight this particular one closes its doors and no one else is allowed in. The place is usually full by six or so anyway.''

A sick feeling curled in Justin's stomach. ''What about Sarah?''

''What about her?''

''What if she's late getting back? Would they let her in? I mean, if she had a good explanation?''

''Sarah's staying at a very good shelter, Justin. Try not to worry. She's been there a couple of weeks now. They've treated her well. They won't turn her out.''

Cold fear filled Justin's heart. ''You're not answering my question. If Sarah was late, would they let her in?''

''Sarah knows the rules. She wouldn't have been late.''

Justin had his answer. ''Thanks, Bill.''

''You okay?''

How could Justin answer that truthfully? ''Yeah,'' he lied.

Sarah, his sister-in-law, who had been here only thirty minutes ago, was living in a shelter. His sister-in-law, for pity sakes! Why hadn't she come to him?

In a flash of insight he realized she had. Today. And he'd snipped at her from the time he'd opened the door, never giving her a chance to state her true purpose in coming.

Anger replaced the guilt. Oh, he'd asked, but she'd refused to tell Justin what was going on. It'd always been that way. Amy had been heartsick when Sarah had closed herself off from her only sister because Amy had married him. Of course Sarah had had a good reason for not speaking to him.

His anger deflated. They were both at fault. But why hadn't she opened up to him tonight and told him she was penniless and living in a shelter?

Because she didn't trust him. And he didn't trust her. And she knew that.

Yet despite that, Justin admitted to his feelings of earlier today. True, he'd felt shock and anger when he'd seen her, then experienced a need to prove that he held nothing against her. But worst of all was the spark of interest he'd felt for her that had slowly made itself known as he'd noticed the sway of her hair, the tilt of her chin, the flash of her eyes.... Self-loathing ate at him. This was Amy's sister, not a woman who should interest him. Especially since he still didn't completely trust her. But all that didn't matter now. The only thing that mattered was that Sarah was living in a shelter.

His sister-in-law.

Mickie's aunt.

There was no way he was going to let her stay there.

"So—" Bill broke the silence "—are you ready to talk?"

Justin sighed. Bill was his friend. He trusted Bill more than anyone else. Maybe he needed to confide in a friend. "I guess at the time of Amy's death Sarah was a convenient person to blame. I was despondent, and according to Sarah, I unintentionally neglected Mickie because of my grief. Maybe Sarah had been acting in Mickie's best interest by taking me to court...or at least she thought she was. I can tell you it certainly woke me up to what was going on around me and that I had a daughter who needed me."

He wondered if Sarah had sensed that things weren't as good between Amy and him as they'd appeared. Had Amy told Sarah she wanted a divorce?

The night of Amy's death, she had admitted that her parents had encouraged the match, saying it was a way of showing the peace between their two families. Had Sarah known or suspected that? He'd been devastated when his wife had run from the house to go see the sister she hadn't talked to in months, because she was tired of trying to "work things out" as he'd insisted they do.

"Amy was angry that every time Sarah and I were near each other we fought. I knew this and tried to curb my tongue, but something got my dander up each time the woman came by. Sarah obviously felt the same way. Amy was caught in the middle and maybe that was why Sarah had fought back the way she did. She had been trying to protect Amy. I just don't know."

Justin ran a weary hand over his face. "She went too far when she tried to take Mickie."

Yes, it had jerked him out of his grief, but the strength he'd found was fueled by anger and hatred, not by God. Things had been disastrous at the trial, breaking the familial bonds between them forever. Or so he'd thought until today, when he'd found out that Sarah was living in a shelter and had tried in her own way to "bury the hatchet."

"You know you can't just go to her and force her to move home with you. If she thinks you're offering her charity she'll disappear. She's a very proud woman."

A very proud woman who was now out wandering the streets because the shelter's doors had closed while she'd been watching Mickie for him. What could he say to Bill? Why hadn't she told him? He had to do something.

An idea formed. Justin would bet that Sarah would be at the shelter tomorrow when the doors opened. She'd been staying there for a while, according to Bill. Yes, his plan just might work.

"Look, Bill, I'm desperate. I need a baby-sitter. I don't know how to get a hold of Sarah. Could you contact her for me tomorrow when the shelter opens for breakfast? Tell her I called looking for her and need her help."

Bill whistled on the other end. "She's gonna go crazy when she finds out you know about her living in a shelter."

"I understand. Maybe you can smooth that over, convince her I'm not handing out charity. My baby-sitter quit tonight and I'm stuck between a rock and a hard place. I need someone—immediately! If it'll help, tell her I'm desperate. You know her better than I do. Do what you have to and convince her to take the job. Call me first thing in the morning after you talk to her."

"Sure thing. And, Justin?"

"Yeah?"

"It's about time you faced this thing between you and Sarah." With those words Bill hung up.

Justin slowly replaced the receiver, trying not to read more into Bill's words than he'd intended. But the truth was, it was hard not to. Because, like a lightning bolt from the sky, he suddenly wondered if maybe that had not been part of the problem all along. Had he married Amy partly out of guilt? Oh, he'd been attracted to her, but what he'd done to her family's business had been part of the equation, too. Unfortunately, she'd married him only out of obligation to her family. He'd cared for Amy. At least on his part he had been willing to stay married forever. They had enjoyed a good comfortable relationship, and in his own way, he'd loved her.

But Bill's words unsettled him more than they should have. Was it not possible that he'd known, on some deeper level, that Amy hadn't loved him and he'd felt threatened by Sarah's anger and dislike?

The possibility was too awful to consider. He didn't want to think that he'd been so insecure back then that he had actually helped cause the wedge in his marriage.

With that thought, he slipped into bed and pulled the covers up to his waist. He would give Sarah a job, prove to her he held no grudges against her and prove to himself that there was really nothing between them at all. Then he'd have his peace again. He could close that part of his life and go forward to face whatever the future held, with no regrets or shadows from the past dogging his heels.

Chapter Three

The doorbell rang, but Justin didn't rush forward the way he wanted to. He didn't throw open the door and greet his sister-in-law with a blast of anger. Instead, he took two repetitive breaths, letting each one out slowly, readying himself for the battle he was sure to face. When he was certain he had control of his emotions, he calmly walked forward and pulled open the door.

She still wore the same jeans from yesterday. She'd changed her shirt, though, he noted. Instead of a white pullover, she wore a pink one.

"Well, are you done gawking at the charity case?"

He raised an eyebrow in silent query, but that only seemed to antagonize her.

"Don't you dare pull that patronizing look on me. It won't work. I've seen it before."

"I'm not trying to be patronizing, Sarah. I just wondered why you were in such a sour mood already this morning. It's not even ten a.m."

She dropped her arms from where she'd crossed them and let them hang at her sides. However, she looked anything but relaxed; she looked ready to pounce on him and take him apart limb by limb.

"You know exactly what's the matter. How could you get Bill involved in this?" she demanded. "He's a friend I trusted, until he hunted me down this morning and told me you had called him last night."

"Is that what's bothering you?"

"No, it's not," she fumed. "What's bothering me is he told you about...well..."

She trailed off and Justin understood it was her lack of a job and an apartment she referred to.

"You offered me work out of pity, and when I told Bill exactly what I thought of that, he told me you refused to take no for an answer and would come to the shelter yourself if I didn't show up here."

So, it had taken the threat of his tracking her down at the homeless shelter to convince her to come to his house this morning. Justin wasn't sure how he felt about that. Insulted? No. A little angry? Maybe. Frustrated? Definitely. But he understood how debasing it must feel for someone she considered her enemy to be offering her a job. However, they were no longer enemies, and the sooner she accepted that, the better.

"Come in." He stepped back. "Mickie is next door playing. She'll be home in a little while."

"Sent her off so she wouldn't see the fireworks?" Sarah replied nastily.

"Yes."

That one word seemed to deflate Sarah. She let out a long sigh, raked a hand through her hair, then finally walked in. Justin didn't wait for her but continued to the kitchen, where he had juice and coffee waiting. He poured her both before hooking a kitchen stool with his foot and pulling it out. Slipping onto it, he indicated the one across from him.

He watched Sarah glance around and wondered what she saw. Little had changed since Amy. The kitchen was still a cozy little place for family meetings.

That's one reason Amy had liked it so much. Modern, with tiles, yellow paint and pale corn-silk flowers on the pastel printed wallpaper, it gave off a feeling of homeyness. A small table for four sat near a picture window that afforded a view of a large backyard and the forest beyond that. The appliances were new, with a small snack bar separating the breakfast area from the actual cooking area.

Did Sarah wonder if he and Amy had eaten their dinner in here or out in the more formal dining room? If they'd had intimate chats in the evening, staring out the window as the sun slowly sank beneath the trees? She was in for a surprise if she thought that.

One of the things Justin truly regretted was there had been none of that. He'd always been too busy to sit down and spend any time with his wife. The melancholy of that inconsideration tried to grab hold of him, but he shook it off. Better to get down to business with Sarah before she decided to get defensive again.

"I need help."

"I've never doubted that."

He smiled at her quick comeback. "My sitter quit. I can't find anyone on such short notice and I have to go to the office today. I'm very picky about whom I leave Mickie with. As you might guess, losing a parent is very hard on a child so small. Even though it's been two years now, Mickie is still not over her mother's death. She needs stability, someone who can be here for her when I'm not.''

Justin fiddled with his coffee cup, staring into the depths of it before raising his gaze back to her.

''I know being a housekeeper-sitter is way beneath your training, but I have a proposition. I want you to work here—live here, too, as a matter of fact. That way, if any emergencies come up and I have to go out of town, someone will be here. The pay is good, but not as good as you would make as a legal assistant. However, while working here, you would be free to send out your résumés and seek a better paying position more in keeping with your experience. All I ask is that any interviews be set up at a time when I'm free to be here with Mickie, and that when you do quit, you give me at least a month's notice so I can find another housekeeper and let Mickie get used to her before you leave.''

Sarah stared at Justin, certain her mouth hung open. In one hand he offered her a job, but only until she could find something else. What did the other hand hold? The hatchet if she blundered? Did he realize how awful his offer sounded? Or had he only been trying to help her and had accidentally made it sound as though he didn't want her around?

Evidently, she'd voiced her opinions, because Justin responded.

''That's not the way I meant it. I simply meant

you'd be doing me a great favor by helping me out. Look, Sarah, I know we never got along before, but you're family. Can we at least try—for Mickie's sake?''

Sarah swallowed. For Mickie's sake? Well, what did she expect? That Justin would say he had been wrong in the past, wrong because of all the pain he had caused her family? He'd come to them and told them he was sorry for what had happened, had even offered compensation and jobs...and married Amy, too. If that didn't show he felt remorseful, what did? But she'd never believed it. She'd thought he should pay for everything that had happened and have no happiness. She'd made it her crusade to make his life miserable, and she had succeeded. If rumor could be believed, he and Amy had been having problems. Amy had never said anything to her, but Sarah wondered now if it was because of all the grief she herself had caused him whenever she was around.

Guiltily, Sarah looked away from the deep brown eyes that stared at her with such intensity. She needed to let go of the past. Wasn't that just the reason she'd come yesterday? Justin was offering to let her look for a job while she worked for him. That was it. Very simple. A way to put the past where it belonged, while proving herself trustworthy.

It galled her, though, to feel that she was taking charity.

As if reading her mind, Justin said quietly, "I'm family, Sarah. Let me help you."

She swallowed her humiliation. She would take the

job, but she would make sure that she earned every penny of her pay. "Very well."

He expelled a great breath. "Fantastic."

When he named her salary her eyes widened in shock. "You can't be serious. That's too much." Her temper rose again. She didn't think housekeepers made that in a month and she didn't like that he thought she was an idiot. After all, how hard could housekeeping and taking care of a child be? She had kept her own house.

"I assure you, Sarah, for cooking, cleaning and taking care of a child, that's the going rate. If you don't believe me, you can call Bill."

Studying him, she decided he was telling the truth. In any event it didn't matter. She was going to make sure she earned her paycheck, with no room for questions.

"Is it a deal?"

"It's a deal."

"Okay. Uh, well, do we need to get clothes, car, anything like that?"

Sarah burned with embarrassment. "Most of my clothes are in a suitcase at the shelter. I do have a few boxes in a storage area that's paid up through next month."

Sarah hated that she'd had to admit such a thing to this man. But he hadn't said anything or given her the slightest reason to think he pitied her. If he had, she would have walked out, despite her desperation for needing the job.

"You can pick them up whenever you're ready." He strode over to a door leading to the garage, where he lifted a key off a hook on a piece of wood shaped like a small house. He brought it back to her. "This is to the car. I'll drive the four-by-four to work—and don't object. We're low on groceries. If you have time today, you'll need to go shopping. Consider free use of my car part of the job." He opened his wallet and pulled out some money.

Sarah's eyes widened.

"This is your first month's salary plus household expenses. The other housekeeper just took the money and as we needed supplies or whatever she paid for them out of an account she'd set up in her own name. There was a box in the office, where she kept all her receipts and stuff. However, if you'd prefer not to have a separate household account, you can buy whatever you feel the house or Mickie needs, then I'll reimburse you."

"No, that's fine. I—I've never done this before. It'll take me a week or two to learn my way around."

"I would expect no less."

"Fine."

"Fine."

They stared at each other for what seemed like minutes before Sarah broke the stare. "Well, I—"

"Sarah," he said softly.

His hand came to rest on her shoulder to keep her from walking away.

"I hope this will be a time to heal for you, me...us. We need to let go of the past and go on."

Sarah couldn't turn around and face him right now. She could not talk about this because she knew her face would give away her feelings. She was attracted to this man. Had she been before her sister had died? She couldn't face that question and certainly couldn't face him as she wondered about it. So instead she simply nodded. ''I agree.''

When she still didn't turn around Justin dropped his hand.

''When will Mickie be home?''

''Any time. I need to go up and change. I have some important work that must be finished today. But let me show you around first.''

Sarah followed but heard little of what Justin actually said. Her mind was on the agreement she'd just made. She would be here for at least one month and she already wondered if this might be a mistake. Would she be able to live in the same house her sister had lived in, with a man who had loved her sister but destroyed her family's business? The same man she found herself undeniably attracted to?

Well, the room definitely reminded Sarah of Amy's taste in decor. Amy had loved greens and yellows.

Sarah walked around the large suite that included a living room and bedroom. Decorated in her sister's favorite colors, it wasn't exactly her taste—she preferred earth tones—but she couldn't deny it was more than she'd had this morning. She could thank God she once again had a roof over her head, even if a man who still despised her had offered it.

Well, Father, she whispered, studying the nice-sized double bed covered in a forest green spread, *Show me what I must do to prove to this man I'm sorry for the past. Help me to restore his trust in me again. It's*

*important that I at least right that wrong so Mickie
won't suffer any pain.*

Sarah wondered again if she was a fool coming here
like this. But when faced with the shocking news of
her infertility and the cruelties of André's family after
he'd left on a trip to sort everything out, she'd suddenly realized how much she regretted breaking off all
contact with Mickie.

True, Amy had married Justin at their parents' urg-
ing, but it was possible she had come to love Justin,
while Sarah had still blamed him for everything that
had happened to her family. She owed it to Amy and
Mickie to try to get to know him.

She remembered that time long ago when she'd first
seen him, how attractive she'd thought him when he'd
come to the office. Then she'd found out he wasn't
one of the underlings from the company that had just
destroyed her parents' lives but the actual owner. He
and his partner had taken over the business. Her
mother had been too torn up to come in and her father
too ill from the shock of losing a business that had
been in the family for a hundred years. As the market
had changed, so had their family changed the goal of
the business. It had been her father's idea to turn the
main part of the organization toward producing computer software components.

When he'd lost the company, he'd suffered a mild
heart attack. Amy hadn't been keen on working in the
office so Sarah had gone in to handle the business until
whatever flunky the new owner would be sending
showed up and officially took over.

The man who arrived hadn't been the rude jerk who

had so cruelly laughed in her father's face when he'd demanded protection for the workers, but a much more handsome, kinder-looking man. But when she'd heard his name…

Sarah shook her head, wondering why she now remembered that she had been the first sister to find this man attractive.

And a few months later, he'd shown up at the door, apologizing for the way the takeover had been handled and offering reimbursement for those who had been let go with no warning.

Her family had been forgiving, willing to welcome him into their house. She hadn't been. They'd had no savings left because of her father's medical bills and because of the bonuses her family had given to help those very families Justin had mentioned. Then, when Justin had asked Amy out, her father had encouraged her to accept his invitations. Her father had formed a grudging but genuine respect for Justin. And perhaps he felt the business might stay in the family if Justin took a liking to Amy and married her, Sarah had often thought.

That had been the beginning of Sarah's separation from her family. She hadn't been able to handle her parents attitude or Amy's submissive acquiescence. She'd moved out almost immediately rather than face Justin and Amy together.

Looking back, Sarah realized part of moving out and breaking off her relations with her family had grown from her horror of the attraction she felt for the man who had, in her opinion, destroyed her family.

While she'd stubbornly hidden herself away, dear

sweet Amy, who had always done exactly as her parents wished, had married Justin.

Now, though, Sarah had to wonder if perhaps Amy hadn't fallen in love with Justin.

Actually, she didn't want to think of that possibility at all. She didn't want to know. She corrected herself. Yes, she *did* want to know but didn't think she'd like the answer. She blushed, aware she shouldn't feel this way unless she was still attracted to the man!

Forcing her mind from those thoughts, she started toward the stairs to start lunch. Justin had said he'd be home by two and she wanted to make sure she couldn't be accused of easing off, even the first day of work.

"I'm home!"

The shout came from downstairs. Sarah smiled. "I'm up here, Mickie."

The little girl came clattering up the stairs. Sarah met her in the hall. Mickie halted abruptly and her expression turned shy. "Where's Daddy?"

"He's at work. Didn't he tell you?"

Mickie twisted her right foot from side to side. "I thought he might be back by now."

Sarah smiled at the little girl and started to reach out for her.

"You left last night without saying goodbye," the little girl admonished, stepping back so she could look Sarah in the eyes.

Sarah blinked, her smile leaving her face. Kneeling in front of Mickie, she took her hands. "That's right. I did. I didn't want to wake you. I'm sorry if it made you sad."

Mickie shrugged. "Mama did the same thing."

Sarah's heart twisted.

Mickie raised her questioning gaze to Sarah's. "Daddy said you're going to be living here. You're going to be the new housekeeper, and you'll make me peanut butter sandwiches with grape jelly. Is that what you were doing up here? Moving in?"

The innocence of children. Sarah nodded. "I'm going to be in the old housekeeper's room in case you ever need anything. And yes, I'll be taking care of you when you're home from school."

She stood and held out her hand. "But I have to wonder if your daddy said that part about grape jelly-and-peanut butter sandwiches."

Mickie wrinkled her freckled little nose. "Well, actually, Daddy said peanut butter sandwiches, but I like the grape jelly so I added that."

Her little hand warmly clasped Sarah's as they started down the stairs. "Well, what if I get you a snack of crackers with peanut butter and grape jelly then I'll make whatever you want for lunch. Your daddy will be back by then and we can have a big meal, then a smaller one tonight."

"You'll be here tonight?"

Sarah didn't pause, though she shuddered at the insecurities the young child must have felt since her mother's death. "I promise." Changing the subject, she asked, "What do you want me to make for dinner?"

In the kitchen she found the peanut butter and set it out with crackers while Mickie found the jelly.

"Fried chicken."

Sarah paused in scooping out the peanut butter into a small bowl. "Fried chicken?" She should have limited her offer to anything baked. She hated frying.

"And a chocolate coconut cake for dessert."

Sarah shook her head ruefully. She should have known. Amy had had a sweet tooth, too. "Well, I can do the fried chicken, but I'm not sure about the cake."

Mickie frowned. She studied the crackers before looking back up at Sarah. "Chocolate coconut cake is my daddy's favorite. The only time he gets it is if he makes it. But he doesn't ever have time. Mommy used to make fried chicken and chocolate coconut cake for dessert. I know Daddy would just love it." She slanted a look up at Sarah. "And so would I."

Sarah sighed. She handed the plate of snacks to Mickie, then poured her a glass of milk. "I'll see what I can do. So, you like coconut, do you?"

Mickie immediately denied it. "I don't. But Daddy does. I just pick it off the top."

So she really was thinking about her daddy. Sarah had thought the child was using a ploy. She still wasn't sure if she was or not. But she found that right now it didn't matter. After taking the chicken from the freezer, she set it in the microwave and punched the buttons to thaw it out. "What's so special about today that you want to fix your daddy's favorite meal."

Mickie shrugged. "He can't cook. I miss Mama's cooking. Can't you cook like her?"

Ah, Sarah thought. Emotions about her sister washed over her. Her sister, the quiet one, the domestic one, the one who had always been so perfect. "Not as well. But if your daddy is starving for good home-cooked meals—'' Sarah winked at Mickie to hide the pain she felt ''—then I suppose I can cook a few good meals for you both.''

Mickie smiled, satisfied.

Relieved, Sarah smiled back. The questions from a five-year-old who would very soon be six—in less than three months, in fact—had been harder than she'd anticipated. Still, it looked as though baby-sitting her was going to be easy. Sarah had survived her first test and had been accepted. How much harder could it be?

Chapter Four

"**W**hat in the world! Mickie, what have you gotten into?"

Sarah stared in horror at the living room and dining room. White powder dusted everything. Following the trail to the dining-room table, she found Mickie standing in a chair with toy cooking utensils, covered in white from head to toe.

"I was making a cake, since you were busy cooking chicken."

Mickie sneezed, then wiped a grimy hand across her face, smearing the white stuff again. She shook her head and a white cloud was released from her formerly brown hair.

"But I told you I'd try to get to it!" Sarah stared blankly at the mess. It was going to take her an hour to clean this up and there was no telling when Justin would be home.

Mickie's shoulders drooped. "I was only trying to help."

Realizing she had hurt Mickie's feelings released Sarah from her inability to react. She went forward and, with only a small reluctance at how dirty she was going to get, gathered Mickie in her arms. "It's okay. Let's go upstairs and run you some bathwater, then I'll clean up the mess."

"I just wanted Daddy to have a cake. He says I'm his little helper."

"It's okay. Really. But maybe next time," Sarah said, going upstairs, "we should do this together. Until you can prove to me you know how," she added, and filled the tub for Mickie.

"Mrs. Winters never would let me. She doesn't like messes."

"Well," Sarah said, stripping the little girl and helping her into the tub, "I don't mind a mess if we do it together. You see, that's the only way to learn. Now, if you promise not to try it by yourself again, maybe next week we can make some cookies together."

Mickie's eyes lit with excitement. "Really?"

"Really."

Sarah quickly washed Mickie's hair, then allowed Mickie to finish up. When she was done, she dried her off. "Can you pick out your clothes by yourself?"

Mickie gave her an exasperated look. "I'm not a baby," she said. "I'll be six January 10."

Sarah bit back a smile. "Of course. I'll be downstairs cleaning up the dining room. The chicken is done. I only have to finish vegetables and potatoes to finish. You can go get out three plates and the silverware while I clean up and finish fixing dinner."

Evidently, Mickie thought she had the better of the two deals, because she didn't argue.

Sarah reentered the dining room and dismally surveyed the white mess. What to do first?

She sighed. Deciding just to wade in, she gathered the play dishes and the tin of flour, which Mickie had somehow sneaked out of the kitchen, and set them all back in their places. After returning to the dining room, she simply swept all the flour onto the floor. Then she wiped down the table and china cabinet and every other piece of furniture that looked to have received a dusting of flour.

Once she'd moved the chairs out of the way, she pulled out the vacuum cleaner and began to vacuum. Mickie came in to set the table. ''Place mats and napkins,'' Sarah said, nodding to where she'd set them out on the beautiful mahogany table.

Sarah had to stop twice to check the potatoes and vegetables she had boiling and then to mash the potatoes.

Then she had to change vacuum bags.

She was getting tired by the time she reached the living room. That was how she explained her accident. Why else would she trip over the vacuum cord, unless all the dusting and vacuuming was tiring her? That and the fact the vacuum cleaner Justin owned weighed almost a ton. He really should have one of those lightweight models, not the monster that made her huff with exertion when using it. Add that to the fact that she hadn't stopped running around since Mickie had entered the house three hours ago and an accident was obviously waiting to happen.

So, it was natural that, as she swept toward the entryway, her shoe tripped her up over the cord.

She squawked in surprise and went flying backward.

Windmilling, grabbing for purchase, Sarah teetered before succumbing to gravity. *I'll probably end up with a broken neck. Then Justin will gloat over just how unfit a parent I would make!*

With one last effort to catch herself before she ended up splitting her head on the floor, she twisted. Instead of ground, a hard dark object arrested her midflight.

The dark object grunted.

In her peripheral vision she saw a briefcase go flying. Strong arms wrapped around her. Her rescuer teetered before both she and her victim continued their fall to the floor.

Splat.

The cessation of noise proved even more telling than her screech when she'd started down.

In the moment it took her to orient herself, she registered several things. The body beside hers was warm and comforting—one arm was still wrapped around her shoulders—and he was in good shape.

She lifted her gaze from the white shirt and tie to Justin's sardonic expression.

She smiled weakly, wondering how to apologize.

He spoke first. "Don't you think you're taking this housekeeping job just a little too seriously?"

"Daddy!"

Hearing Mickie's voice, Sarah immediately scrambled off Justin. "I'm so sorry. We had a little accident and I was sweeping. I wasn't paying attention to where I was going and got tangled up in the cord."

He stood, dusted off his suit, then scooped Mickie up in his arms. "Hiya, pumpkin," he said, bussing her cheek.

Sarah winced at how Mickie was dressed. Blue striped shorts with an orange checked top. Justin blinked, cast a glance at Sarah, then returned his attention to Mickie.

She squeezed his neck. "Sarah made your favorite meal but we didn't have time to bake a cake. I tried but made a mess, instead, and Aunt Sarah cleaned it up while I set the table."

Justin raised an eyebrow and scanned the room. He hugged Mickie again before setting her down. "My favorite meal, huh?" He made a big show of sniffing the air. "Fried chicken?"

Mickie laughed and nodded.

"That's great! Go upstairs and wash up. Let me get my briefcase and change. Then we'll eat."

Mickie immediately ran upstairs.

Justin gathered the contents of his briefcase and Sarah belatedly helped him. "So what's the special occasion?" he asked as he snapped the lid shut.

Sarah fidgeted. She hadn't expected to be questioned on what she had prepared. "I told Mickie I'd make her anything she wanted. And fried chicken with chocolate coconut cake was her choice."

An indefinable emotion crossed Justin's features before he sighed.

"Did I do something wrong?" Sarah asked, ill at ease with the unnamed emotion she'd seen.

"No." He shook his head.

"I know Mickie was young when Amy died, but she still remembers Amy in her own way. Certain things stand out in her mind, while others have faded. But one thing she remembers is one of the last big meals Amy, Mickie and I shared together as a family. It was fried chicken and a cake for dessert. Amy had made it for my birthday. It's not that it's my favorite, though I do love chicken. But in her mind…"

He trailed off.

Sarah understood. "Children remember things differently. I suppose remembering the special times is her way of holding on to Amy."

Justin nodded. "Mickie had a bad experience with the last housekeeper. The woman flat refused to fry food. She said it was bad for her. So the only time Mickie got fried chicken was when I fried it on the housekeeper's day off. I couldn't figure out for a long while why she wanted fried chicken until one day she told me it was my favorite. The story came out and I started seeing to it that we had it whenever Mickie requested it."

Justin went to the entry closet and placed his briefcase in there. "The only time she asks for it is when she's feeling insecure or sad."

Sarah looked down at her hands. "Do you think I triggered her sudden insecurity?"

Justin sighed. "It's possible. You knew Amy. Mickie has really been missing her mom lately. Maybe she just needs to be reassured that some things will stay the same."

"You know, I think I need to mention I hurt her

last night leaving without waking her up. She said her mom did the same thing.''

A spasm of pain crossed his face. "Yeah. Amy and I had a fight. When she left, she flew out of the house. Mickie was asleep.''

"She also asked if I could cook like Amy.''

Justin dropped his head back and stared at the ceiling. Finally, he said, "I'm sorry, Sarah. Mickie doesn't understand other people's pain. She's only a child.''

Sarah bristled. "I know that. I just thought maybe, well…to me, I guessed that she was missing her mom. I told her I'd try to make homemade meals like Amy, though I'm not as good a cook.''

Justin nodded. "Thank you.''

He turned and started up the stairs. Sarah stared after him, noting how wide his shoulders were. Wide enough to have carried the burden of losing his wife and being a single parent alone? Or had he depended on God to help him?

Sarah remembered his confessions of salvation and that was why he had changed his tune about so many things he'd always considered *woman* things. Her mother had insisted Justin had never been underhanded in business, but that after he'd been saved, Justin had felt the need to make restitution for things that had happened during the takeover, things Justin hadn't known about.

Justin disappeared from sight and she sighed. She really didn't want to remember how her parents had insisted Justin was a nice guy. She only wanted to be friends, make up for her past; not continue to feel

guilty as more and more facets of his giving personality revealed themselves to show him as a truly caring
man and loving father.

She went to the kitchen and brought out the food.
Just as she carried in the glasses of iced tea, Justin and
Mickie appeared. Mickie wore pink leggings and a
sweatshirt with Daisy Duck on the front. Her outfit not
only matched, but it suited the nippy weather outside.

Once seated, they offered thanks for the meal, then
passed the food around the table. "So, Sarah, what are
you doing for Thanksgiving?"

Sarah flushed and paused only a moment before
passing the potatoes to Justin. When he took them
from her, she reluctantly met his eyes. She saw in his
gaze that he knew she had no family and he'd hurt her
by asking. But what could she say? Her fiancé had
planned for her to spend Thanksgiving at his house.
But that was before he'd told her he was taking a
couple of months off to think, before the letter from
Watson and Watson had made it clear she was fired—
because André hadn't had the guts to tell her himself.
"I don't know. Maybe—"

"How about you spend it here," Justin interrupted,
dishing some potatoes up for Mickie. "We don't have
anyone else coming. Bill usually stops by. I don't
know what he'll do now that he's married. But we'd
love to have you."

Mickie, ever tuned in to any conversation around
her, piped up, "Please, Aunt Sarah. And this year we
could have a real turkey instead of the one Daddy buys
at the store. It was too chewy," she added, making
a face.

It was Justin's turn to flush. "Hey, kiddo," he warned good-naturedly, "it was either chewy turkey or going out to a restaurant. And I happen to like eating at home on a holiday, so we just might order chewy turkey again this year."

"But you got cherry pie for dessert."

Sarah chuckled. "Well, maybe I could make up a pumpkin."

Mickie wrinkled her nose in disgust.

"Or chocolate?"

Mickie grinned.

"Does that mean I've convinced you?" Justin asked, smiling.

She grinned. "Someone has convinced me...I think the part about picking up the meal held sway."

Justin's smile deepened and Sarah suddenly felt awkward. Clearing her throat, she began to eat.

After a few minutes of silence, Justin asked, "What are your plans for today?"

Sarah shrugged. "I definitely need to go shopping. I thought I'd get some boxes from storage." She sipped her tea, then plunged ahead. "You won't mind watching Mickie the rest of today, will you? I'll be back by dinner."

Sarah wanted time away from the domestic scene so she could come to grips with all the changes since arriving at the house. It seemed that her whole life had been turned upside down in one short day.

Sarah looked up, expecting a frown. After all, Justin had promised her Sunday to herself if she wanted it, not Saturday, and she wasn't even sure he was done with all his work. Instead, a knowing smile met her.

"I don't mind spending the day with Mickie for a minute. But if you think I'm going to let you work all day while we play..." He tsked. "I suggest we go with you so I can help load those boxes, then we'll all grab something for supper on the way home."

"No, really," she started to protest.

Justin stopped her by shaking his head. "I insist. Besides, it's Saturday. Saturday is supposed to be a fun day, isn't it, Mickie?"

Mickie squealed and immediately launched into what their Saturdays were usually like.

As Mickie rambled on, Justin smiled tenderly. Sarah, however, didn't hear what Mickie was saying.

Because when Justin turned that smile on her, she realized with a sinking heart that his smile was the true reason she wanted out of there for a while.

Chapter Five

"I have to say, this is the most interesting supper I've ever had."

Justin laughed and leaned his forearms on the picnic table at the local park where he'd taken Sarah and Mickie.

Sarah marveled at how comfortable he looked in his jeans and flax-colored blazer. She imagined he could wear a three-piece suit out here and still look just as relaxed as long as Mickie was around.

Glancing to the slide, she heard Mickie's squeal just as she came into view again. Ruefully, she shook her head. "I don't know how she can twist around in that thing right after eating and not get sick."

"She's always had that ability. I, on the other hand," Justin said, "feel queasy just watching her."

Sarah gathered up the plastic containers that had held their salads and sandwiches and took them over to the trash can.

When she was again seated by Justin, she noted his

smile was pensive, possibly wistful. "There're not many warm days left for her to enjoy."

She was amazed, actually, that Justin had taken time to stop at a playground and allow Mickie to play. Of course, she shouldn't be surprised. He was so different from the man she remembered. "Has it been hard?" she asked, voicing her thoughts. As soon as she realized what she'd said she wanted to grab the words back, but it was too late. She swallowed. "I'm sorry, Justin. I have no right—"

"No, it's okay." He watched Mickie climb up the slide and come swirling down again before he answered. "Yeah, in many ways it has been, I suppose. It took some adjusting to being the only one for her to run to when she was hurt or excited or just wanted to talk. One of the most memorable adjustments was in buying her clothes and teaching her so many things."

He sighed, and Sarah could see how serious his eyes were as he looked into himself.

"I guess that has actually been the hardest—those things we traditionally think of as mother-daughter things. You know, the playing in the kitchen as she would have while watching her mom cook. Or even the special Mother Day's activities and school functions where the mothers are asked to attend. And the little everyday messes kids get into that moms handle."

"Like what?"

He smiled. "I can remember some of the messes my sister, Diode, got into. Though she's a missionary overseas now and I haven't seen her in four years I think about her a lot because of Mickie. I see Mickie and realize she'll never have the fun of playing dress-up in her mom's clothes the way Diode did or the forays into Mom's makeup or her perfumes. Then, of course, fixing Mom her Mother's Day breakfast.''

He had a wistful smile as he spoke of those times, Sarah noted, smiling herself.

Mickie squealed. Both Sarah and Justin glanced up to see if she was okay. When they were assured she was safe, Justin continued. ''I think the hardest is knowing she misses Amy. She'll be fine some days. Then there are times when I see her playing and I can tell she's thinking about her mommy.''

''Does she talk about Amy a lot?''

Justin shook his head. ''Only occasionally.''

He lapsed into silence. The sound of the oak trees echoed loudly in the silence, as did the rumble of an occasional car on the nearby highway. Several mothers with their children sat around at other picnic tables and a sporadic laugh could be heard. But since the three of them were on the other side of the park, an air of isolation permeated their table.

''I miss her,'' he finally said.

She felt Justin studying her but wouldn't meet his eyes. ''At first I was angry that she left, but now there's only sadness and good memories. I guess we just have to let go and get on with our lives.''

Coming to terms had been hard for Justin. She remembered the grief he'd experienced when she'd finally decided to take Mickie away from him.

''Where was she going that night?'' Sarah asked. It was the first time they'd ever really talked about

Amy's death. It felt so good, a cleansing of her soul, to at last be able to ask the questions she had wanted to ask for years.

Justin stiffened. His face turned dark. "I suppose you have a right to know. She was coming to see you. You see, she had decided to leave me."

"Divorce?" Amy almost fell off the bench. Her family hadn't believed in divorce. Amy had always been the perfect one, the one to follow all the rules set by her parents. "But why?"

He shrugged as though it didn't matter. But Sarah had a feeling it mattered very much if the way his features had gone so blank was any indication. "I'm sure you know your parents pushed the match."

Sarah glanced down, embarrassed. Oh, yes, she'd known that. "She came to love you."

"I don't think so. You see, the night she left me, she told me she was tired of living a sham her parents had forced her into. She couldn't handle the unreality of what we had and she was tired of not having a sister or experiencing any of the things she'd one day hoped to experience when she was out of her family's house. So she left, telling me we would talk about custody later."

Sarah was dizzy. Amy had said that? Her sister, Amy?

"Maybe it was just a remark in the heat of the moment," Sarah offered weakly.

Again, Justin shook his head. "I should have realized she was unhappy. It's just that I'd become settled in the relationship and loved her, and was certain her love would grow. I hoped she was just shy, then maybe undemonstrative. Finally, I decided she just didn't like to show emotion.''

He stretched as if he didn't have a care in the world, but Sarah knew different. Justin was still hurting over the pain her sister had inflicted the night before she'd run from him. How she knew that, she wasn't sure. But she knew Justin blamed himself for Amy's death as much as for marrying Amy when she hadn't really loved him. His next words confirmed her fears.

''You know, I sometimes wonder if there was something I could have done differently—''

''No, Justin. Don't ever second-guess the past.''

''Why not?'' he asked, bitterness in his voice.

Turning her face toward Mickie, she said, ''Because if we're going to second-guess, then we'll need to remember that I was her sister and I'm the one who acted like a spoiled child and broke off contact with the family. Had I been there for Amy to talk to, she might not have buried so many unresolved things inside her until she felt she had to leave to solve them.''

Though she said it, she wondered why her sister hadn't poured her heart out to God and allowed God to help her through her struggle. Of course, Amy had never liked confrontation of any sort. That was why she'd always done what her mother and father had told her to—unlike Sarah. ''If I hadn't been so filled with bitterness and anger...'' She shrugged.

Justin suddenly deflated. ''That's how I felt about my partner. He'd been like a brother to me. I couldn't believe it when I found out all the underhanded things he was into. It took God's infinite patience to teach me to forgive and let go of my bitterness. Actually, through that fiasco He taught me just how important forgiveness is.''

Yes, he'd asked Jesus into his heart just after that, Sarah mused. She wondered if he'd forgiven her as easily, or if he still harbored pain and bitterness.

But instead of asking, she offered, ''I learned that problems with work or other earthly matters seem unimportant compared with relationships like family. There are always going to be problems, but not always family. I just wish it hadn't taken so long for me to learn after I'd lost all my family.''

Justin finally turned to her and she saw compassion in his eyes.

''But you didn't, Sarah. You still have Mickie.''

Her heart flipped over at his words and the tenderness in his eyes. What could she say to that? Or to the very warm look he was giving her?

''Daddy, come push me!''

Relieved that she didn't have to reply, Sarah turned her attention to Mickie, who was climbing onto one of the swings near their table.

Justin stood, obviously as relieved to have the dark discussion over as she was. ''Okay, pumpkin, hang on tight,'' he warned, and strolled to where Mickie was already giggling and kicking her legs back and forth in excitement.

''High, Daddy, high!''

Justin grabbed the swing and pushed, sending her into a slow arc. ''Higher, higher!'' she cried, swinging her legs and laughing.

Sarah couldn't resist walking closer. Their laughter was infectious. She watched Justin, enthralled by how handsome he looked as he threw back his head and laughed.

Sarah wasn't prepared for when his gaze met hers, or for the gleam in his eye. "You know, Mickie, I think Aunt Sarah would enjoy being pushed, too. What do you think?"

"Oh, no, I don't think—"

"Yes! Oh, yes, Daddy. Push Sarah, too." Mickie looked from where she was still swinging. "He won't let you fall."

"Come on, Sarah," Justin entreated, smiling. He motioned to the swing. "Trust me."

With both of them encouraging her, how could she refuse? Wary, she approached the other swing. The sand shifted under her flats and she walked carefully, attempting to keep her balance on the shifting surface. "It's been years since I've been in a swing," she warned.

"Years?" Mickie asked in obvious horror.

"That's too long," Justin said.

Sarah felt him approaching. "Oh, I don't need to be pushed, too," she objected.

Then his hands closed over the chains on each side of her waist. His warm breath tickled her neck and his musky aftershave filled her senses. Sarah shivered in reaction and was appalled. She'd just been engaged. She could not be enjoying how close he stood to her. She wasn't even sure he had forgiven her!

She had no more time to think, as suddenly he pulled back her swing, then let loose. She gasped in dismay, then delight. She'd forgotten how free swinging felt, the weightless quality, the air rushing through her hair.

Then she was back, and Justin's strong hands pushed again, sending her even higher.

Sarah shrieked. His low laugh joined Mickie's as he alternated pushing them. "Stop that, Justin," she warned, when he again gave her swing a hard push. But there was no heat in her words. Indeed, laughter bubbled out.

"Stop what?" he asked innocently, and continued right along.

"You know very well what," she said, casting a glance at Mickie, who was high in the air, her eyes closed, her squeals pealing out over the area.

"Get off if you don't like it," he taunted, chuckling.

The sound sent warm tingles over her nerves.

"I don't remember how to stop it!" she cried, but there was pleasure in her voice and she knew he heard it in the way his laugh rumbled again.

Sarah quickly relearned how to use her legs to propel herself forward. Justin climbed into another swing and swung, too, making outrageous faces at Mickie and Sarah as he passed them.

She thoroughly enjoyed herself. No man had ever teased or played with her the way Justin did. It was a new and delightful experience. It'd been years since she'd acted like a kid. But she found she loved it.

Was that something Justin had learned since Amy's death? How to enjoy his daughter and have fun? Or had he been like that before and she'd just never known?

She knew Justin certainly had a way of making a

woman feel feminine. Whether he realized it or not, the looks he'd given her today and the way he was so careful as he pushed her even when he was playing made her feel womanly, cherished and treated with regard. It was a nice feeling. One she really enjoyed. How long had it been since she'd enjoyed life? Since her fiancé? Or before?

"How do I stop this thing?" Sarah asked, deciding it was time to get off.

Justin jumped from his swing. "Right here," he said, and held out his arms.

"Oh, yeah, sure," she replied, and rolled her eyes.

He raised an eyebrow arrogantly. Turning toward Mickie, he held out his arms. "Let's show her, Mickie," he said, then broke eye contact and met his daughter's gleeful gaze.

"Here I come, Daddy!" She flew off the swing. Before Sarah could scream in fear, Mickie landed safely in his arms.

"Your turn," he said, and held out his arms.

"You're crazy," she replied, and kicked again, thinking to plant her feet in the sand and stop herself. So what if she would probably go face first into the dirt. She wasn't ready to jump into someone's arms.

"Chicken?" he taunted, his arms folded across his chest.

Her chin jutted out. Had he figured her out so quickly? Did he know that she wanted to trust him but feared it? She stared at him.

What would it hurt? It just might be fun, flying through the air and landing in Justin's embrace. With only a moment's hesitation, she decided. "Don't blame me if you break a few bones."

He held out his arms. She swung forward but all of a sudden found that her hands wouldn't release the chains. Justin was big, but was he big enough to hold her? She swung forward a second time. Was this really fun? She wondered as her hands began to sweat.

But it was Justin's smug look that goaded her into acting. She came forward again and pushed out of the swing. True, it was only a few feet, but it felt like miles before she thudded into Justin.

Strong arms wrapped around her, jarring her to a stop. Immediately, Justin pulled her closer toward his powerful, hard chest. His scent, as well as an extreme feeling of safety and security, enveloped her. She rested her cheek against his shoulder for an instant, surprised at her reaction, then pulled back.

In that moment, things changed. The world tilted just a bit—or maybe it was her. Because she suddenly realized just how attracted she was to Justin, more attracted than she'd been to her fiancé, or to any other man she'd ever dated. And there was nothing she could do about it, because Justin was the very man she'd tried to destroy two years ago.

Justin saw Sarah's eyes widen, then how she backed away. He was thankful she had put some distance between them, because he was afraid he might have just kissed her.

He hadn't thought about dating in ages. Oh, true, women approached him—pleasant, attractive women he met through business or at church—but he'd never been tempted in the least to pursue any of them. Earlier today, though, and now again…what was it about Sarah that was different from all the others? She brought out a surge of protectiveness and tenderness, true. He wanted to hold her and shield her. But why? Why her? His feelings were disconcerting, embarrassing.

Hearing Mickie's laughter, he wondered what his daughter would have thought if he'd kissed Sarah just now. He shook his head, feeling an emotion churning in his gut.

Loneliness.

He had to admit he was lonely. He loved his daughter, and Bill was a great guy. But Justin missed having someone closer around to share his experiences with. There was no one to talk to in the evening when he got home from work, no one to laugh together with over a joke or share those little secret smiles when Mickie did something really adorable. There was no one to hold when he felt overwhelmed or to love when he wanted to share that special experience.

But Sarah?

No.

He couldn't see himself with his sister-in-law, who probably still despised him despite what she said. Besides, he thought, going over to the picnic table where Mickie was slurping her cola, he would never risk entering into a marriage for convenience's sake, or for an attraction, either. He'd learned his lesson. Convenience could turn into inconvenience real quick, and passion could fade.

Odd though it sounded, he had vowed to marry only for love.

His lips twisted cynically. People always thought women were the romantic ones, yet here he was, insisting on a love-based marriage. And how many women in the past two years had hinted at so many other types of arrangements. Love based, with him? Not one woman who had shown an interest had wanted love. Sarah certainly wouldn't fall into that category, either...would she?

Hah.

He skeptically wondered if any women out there still believed in a marriage based on love.

Reaching his daughter's side, he realized Sarah was wiping up some cola Mickie had spilled on her top. His gaze settled on Sarah and against his will, he had to wonder why *love* and *Sarah* had come to him in the same thought.

Chapter Six

"I hope you decide to spend Thanksgiving with us."

"I'd enjoy it," Sarah replied.

It was dark. Mickie was asleep in the back seat and Sarah rested her head against the cushion of her seat in Justin's car.

But she was far from relaxed. Tumultuous emotions over the day spent at the park still filled her thoughts. After the swings, Justin had proceeded to push Mickie, and several other children, on a merry-go-round. Then he'd actually gone down one of the tamer slides with his daughter. They'd played until all three were exhausted and the sun had set.

Sarah couldn't remember enjoying a sunset more. Then they'd piled into the car to head home.

With the darkness surrounding them, and the peace and quiet, Sarah had had time to remember her reaction to Justin early that day. Tension built in the small enclosed space between the two of them until she could barely stand it.

...n he spoke, it was a relief to have her mind on

...keep the subject on some-
...kie like that often?''
with Mickie.
...ldren.''

wiggled be-
as she watched
Sarah went to the
...bles. She marveled
...en was. Amy had al-
...e refrigerator was clean
...here the fresh vegetables
she'd make a salad with
dinner. Maybe she ought to do
...stin's approval each week first.
...not eat some of the same things

mental note to ask him about that.
...er realize she might not know as mu...
...eeping as she thought.
...d-black baskets hung over the counte...
...gerator. One had potatoes and an oni...
...rator in that one, then unloaded the
...er basket. Bananas, tangelos, orang...
...les—Mickie certainly liked fruit.
Two boxes of cereal went on top
She looked at them and frowned ov...

"You're the boss," she murmured, and followed him to the house. She smiled over how wonderful he was with Mickie. Her sleepy little head lay against hi. left shoulder and her legs and arms surrounded h like a monkey holding on to its mom. Long curl covered her face and flowed over Justin's blaz could hear him murmuring something in girl's ear as he opened the door.

A small sigh escaped Mickie and she fore letting out a half snore.

Tenderness welled in Sarah's hear Justin carry the child up the stairs. kitchen and put away the veget again at how beautiful the kitc ways had wonderful taste. Th and it was easy to find w went. Perhaps tomorrow stuffed bell peppers for up a menu and get J After all, he might she did.

She made a Which made about house

Brass-a the refri *She p* frige oth

She
get the b
me back out for
ts or dairy products.
shrugged as he lifted his
kie doesn't get to go to the playe
to spend time with her today."

Chapter Six

"I hope you decide to spend Thanksgiving with us."

"I'd enjoy it," Sarah replied.

It was dark. Mickie was asleep in the back seat and Sarah rested her head against the cushion of her seat in Justin's car.

But she was far from relaxed. Tumultuous emotions over the day spent at the park still filled her thoughts. After the swings, Justin had proceeded to push Mickie, and several other children, on a merry-go-round. Then he'd actually gone down one of the tamer slides with his daughter. They'd played until all three were exhausted and the sun had set.

Sarah couldn't remember enjoying a sunset more. Then they'd piled into the car to head home.

With the darkness surrounding them, and the peace and quiet, Sarah had had time to remember her reaction to Justin early that day. Tension built in the small enclosed space between the two of them until she could barely stand it.

His lips twisted cynically. People always thought women were the romantic ones, yet here he was, insisting on a love-based marriage. And how many women in the past two years had hinted at so many other types of arrangements. Love based, with him? Not one woman who had shown an interest had wanted love. Sarah certainly wouldn't fall into that category, either...would she?

Hah.

He skeptically wondered if any women out there still believed in a marriage based on love.

Reaching his daughter's side, he realized Sarah was wiping up some cola Mickie had spilled on her top. His gaze settled on Sarah and against his will, he had to wonder why *love* and *Sarah* had come to him in the same thought.

When he spoke, it was a relief to have her mind on something else.

"I enjoyed today."

Of course he wouldn't keep the subject on something safe. "Do you play with Mickie like that often?"

"As much as I can. I love playing with Mickie. Sometimes I wish Amy and I had had more children." Sarah silently winced at his admission, but did her best to hide it.

"Did you have fun today, Sarah?"

"Yes, I did," she replied. "I just don't feel I'm earning my pay."

He chuckled. "Consider it part of your job to play with Mickie. After all, you're going to find Mickie is a very active child. And I can just about guarantee that you won't think you're not earning your pay after a week or two living here."

The headlights cut across the front of the house when they turned into the driveway, and Sarah realized they were home.

Justin stopped the car, then pushed open his door. Sarah blinked at the light, suddenly realizing she was tired.

"I'll unload the car later. Just grab the fruit and vegetables."

She reached in for the two bags, debating whether to get the boxed and canned goods or allow Justin to come back out for them. "I see now why you said no meats or dairy products."

He shrugged as he lifted his daughter into his arms. "Mickie doesn't get to go to the playground much. I wanted to spend time with her today."

''You're the boss,'' she murmured, and followed him to the house. She smiled over how wonderful he was with Mickie. Her sleepy little head lay against his left shoulder and her legs and arms surrounded him like a monkey holding on to its mom. Long curly hair covered her face and flowed over Justin's blazer. She could hear him murmuring something in the little girl's ear as he opened the door.

A small sigh escaped Mickie and she wiggled before letting out a half snore.

Tenderness welled in Sarah's heart as she watched Justin carry the child up the stairs. Sarah went to the kitchen and put away the vegetables. She marveled again at how beautiful the kitchen was. Amy had always had wonderful taste. The refrigerator was clean and it was easy to find where the fresh vegetables went. Perhaps tomorrow she'd make a salad with stuffed bell peppers for dinner. Maybe she ought to do up a menu and get Justin's approval each week first. After all, he might not eat some of the same things she did.

She made a mental note to ask him about that. Which made her realize she might not know as much about housekeeping as she thought.

Brass-and-black baskets hung over the counter near the refrigerator. One had potatoes and an onion in it. She put the other vegetables that didn't go in the refrigerator in that one, then unloaded the fruit in the other basket. Bananas, tangelos, oranges, yellow apples—Mickie certainly liked fruit.

Two boxes of cereal went on top of the refrigerator. She looked at them and frowned over one. White sugar. If Mickie was active, as Justin had intimated, Sarah was sure she'd just found the culprit. When had Justin slipped that into the basket without her seeing?

Of course, Justin could have slipped anything into the basket and she would have missed it. She'd been feeling so inept around him that she hadn't paid attention to everything he had grabbed. And Mickie had been talking, too. She certainly could talk. Though Sarah didn't consider that a bad habit. It was wonderful listening to everything from her perspective.

Just as she finished putting away the eggs and bread, alarm swept through Sarah. She hadn't said good-night to Mickie. She folded the paper bags and placed them under the sink. Whether they were kept there or not, she wasn't sure. But it was where she'd always stored her bags. Then she hurried up the stairs and quickly headed to Mickie's room.

And almost ran Justin down.

She flushed and took a step back.

"What's the rush?" he asked, smiling down at her.

Sarah saw Justin had a frilly little nightie in his hand. She found the idea of him dressing Mickie funny. In her mind, dressing a child for bed had always been a mother's role. But, she thought, sobering, of course he would do it. Mickie no longer had a mother. "I forgot to tell Mickie good-night."

He looked confused only for a moment, then what she thought was tenderness—but couldn't be sure—touched his eyes. How unusual. He was so big. Tall with broad shoulders. Towering over her. She'd always assumed he was gruff and belligerent, the way she'd always perceived him when in his company. To think that Justin could feel tenderness was just so out of keeping with the way she'd always imagined him. But she was almost certain that was what she'd seen in his eyes earlier today and again just now.

Feeling even more uncomfortable from that innocent revelation, she hurriedly said, "I promised Mickie I'd always make sure to tell her good-night so she'd know I hadn't left."

He stared at her a moment more and those feelings from earlier today resurfaced: need, wanting, longing.

Justin cleared his throat, the feelings in his gaze suddenly banked. He stepped back. "I was getting ready to put her in her p.j.'s. She can bathe tomorrow, since she's already asleep." He held out an arm, indicating an area just inside the door off to the side. "Come in."

He stepped back and Sarah stepped in. She liked Mickie's room. It had a nice feeling. The walls were a light blue. Colored balloons and painted pieces of cardboard cut in the shape of stars covered the surfaces. There were also pictures of different cartoon characters on the walls, cut out of magazines, as well as many copies of Sunday-school literature taped up on the wall with pictures of Jesus and other biblical figures in them.

Like most little girls her age, Mickie liked clutter. And she had varying taste, if the pictures were any indication. Stepping over the dolls and the teddy bears, Sarah made her way to the side of the bed.

"Today is usually the day she cleans her room— every Saturday, unless we do something special," Justin explained.

"I was messy as a child," Sarah admitted. She was very conscious of Justin as he followed her over to where Mickie lay.

She sat down on the edge of the bed and stared at the sleeping child. "She sure is still," Sarah murmured.

A chuckle sounded behind her. "The only time she's still is when she's asleep," Justin replied.

Smoothing a strand of hair from Mickie's face, she leaned down and kissed the soft, pale cheek. "Good night, sweet princess," she teased, thinking Mickie already had her wrapped around her little finger.

She stood, nodded to Justin and attempted to make a quick escape.

But she wasn't fast enough.

"Sarah?" Justin called just as she got to the doorway.

She paused, then turned. "Yes?"

"Thanks for coming back into our lives."

Awkwardly, she nodded.

What could she say? Once she was in her room, she grabbed some clothes and went to the bathroom to shower. His words continued to echo in her head. *Thanks for coming back into our lives.* How could he say that? Especially after what she'd done? She remembered the shock and anger when she'd told him she wanted Mickie, that he wasn't a fit father. Then she remembered the steely determination when he'd faced her in court that day. Gone had been the thin, gaunt-cheeked man who had seemed so listless, so remote. In his place was a man wearing a designer suit, a man armed with a lawyer who had glanced at her across the courtroom with a pitying look. Of course she hadn't known then what Justin's lawyer was about to present to the court. Justin had definitely gone all out and found the best lawyer for the job.

Her lawyer had scrambled and tried to help her. But of course grief had been accepted as Justin's excuse, and expert witnesses testified that he had gotten through the worst of his mourning and on and on and on. She had been furious, believing Mickie belonged with her, that Justin was neglecting his daughter.

But her fury had been minor compared with Justin's when he'd told her never to come near his daughter again. She had actually felt chilled at his threats.

That seemed like aeons ago. And Justin acted as if he'd forgiven her.

She rinsed her hair, stepped out of the shower and dried off. Perhaps he just needed a sitter. But why would he be glad she was back in his life unless he had forgiven her?

She smoothed cream on her skin, then powdered herself before applying a spritz of perfume. She'd always loved to pamper herself after her bath. All three containers were almost empty, leftovers from her other life, as she thought of her life before her job and engagement ended. But she'd have some money now to indulge her one luxury.

Still, as she gathered up her toiletries, she thought of the person providing her with the paycheck.

How could he forgive her? Why? Why? Why? And why had he let her into his house?

Back in her room, she put her things away, turned out the lights, opened the curtains, then climbed up onto the big four-poster bed. *Father, Justin's so wonderful as a dad,* she began. *I never realized it. I was so wrong in my judgment of him. There's no way he can forget what I did. Is there? I doubt I'll ever forget it.*

Sarah sighed and pulled the white lacy pillow into her lap, then clung to it. *How can I,* she whispered finally, admitting to the enormity of what she'd done, *when it was Amy I wronged as well as Justin? And then there's Mickie.*

Sarah slipped under the covers and scooted back against the headboard. The darkness surrounded her; the only light in her room the moonlight that shone through the windows. A small smile curved her mouth and she relaxed as she thought of Mickie.

Thank you, Father, for the opportunity to get to know Mickie. Had You not interceded, I don't know if I'd ever have gotten up the nerve to come visit her. She's wonderful. She's so sweet and kind and fun. She's so fresh and innocent. Sarah felt old and weary next to Mickie's innocence, but she didn't say that. *I missed Amy's companionship and didn't know how much I was missing out on getting to know her daughter. Thank you, Father, for Your love and for Your gentleness and kindness. Help me to be what Mickie and Justin need.*

Sighing, she slid down in bed. *Despite the pain of losing my fiancé, I'm happy now. I realize I had drifted from You and hadn't cleared up my past. Give me courage to make up to Justin for the wrongs I paid him. And, Father, I just know this is going to work out great with Mickie! Despite what Justin says, Mickie seems like the perfect little girl. I really don't think I'm going to have problems there. Just, maybe, the housekeeping part. So give Justin patience as I learn exactly when he likes to eat and things like that. Amen.*

Feeling better after praying, she smiled as she closed her eyes. She would be a good housekeeper and a caring companion for Mickie. Things weren't going to be so bad after all.

Chapter Seven

"It's a Sarah Connelly on the line, Mr. Warner."

Justin pushed back from the paperwork he'd been working on. Brushing a hand through his hair, he leaned forward and snagged the phone.

"Sarah?" he questioned. She'd been baby-sitting for him for over a week now and had never called him at the office. He couldn't imagine what in the world she'd phone him for, unless it was an emergency.

"I can't find her!"

The panicked voice sent a chill down his spine. "Find her? Find who, Sarah? Mickie?"

"Yes. School got out early today. You know that. But she had a tutoring session and I was trying to make that cake she wanted and time got away from me."

The chill turned to full-blown alarm. "Go on," he said, despite the fact he was certain he heard her snif-fle. "Tell me."

"I was only ten minutes late. I rushed up to the

school. A few children were still around, so it wasn't as though I was *that* late. But she wasn't there.''

Terror gripped his heart, but he forced it down. Sarah was hysterical enough for both of them. ''What did the principal say?''

''I didn't ask her. The teacher outside said she had just seen Mickie in the line but didn't notice her leave the school yard. I started tracing the route home, thinking she might have walked, but couldn't find her. I went back up to the school. I've even been home. She's nowhere. I thought about calling the police—''

''Mr. Warner?''

He waved at his secretary, motioning her out, but she came forward. ''Mr. Warner, Stephanie Williams is on the phone. It's about Mickie.''

His gaze snapped up at those words. Relief and a sudden suspicion filled his mind. ''Sarah, hold on a minute. I may have found Mickie.''

He punched the other line, feeling the tension increase. ''Ms. Williams?''

A trilling laugh floated over the phone line. ''I've told you a dozen times to call me Stephanie, Mr. Warner.''

''My secretary said it's about Mickie,'' he interrupted, feeling his already frayed temper slipping even further from his control.

''Why, yes, it is. Why, the poor little dear. You know I volunteer up there three days a week. I stayed after to help test some of the slower children today during tutoring. You know, they had tutoring today. Anyway...''

Justin wished he could rip the words out of her, but

Stephanie had her own way of telling a story and a talent for drawing the attention to herself. Already, though, his body was relaxing. Mickie was with Stephanie. Somehow he just knew it.

"Yes?" he questioned when she didn't continue.

"I was getting ready to bring my own child home and Mickie was still there. I had a feeling she was thinking about walking home the way she kept looking around for her ride. The poor little dear. I know you've been having trouble with baby-sitters, so I asked her if anyone was coming to pick her up. She said her aunt Sarah had forgotten her. I didn't know you had a sister. I insisted she ride home with me and we'd call as soon as we arrived, but we forgot, having our cookies and milk, so I'm calling you now."

Justin closed his eyes and counted to ten. Stephanie wanted him as her next husband. She'd done just about everything to get the message across except send him a telegram. She loved his house, his money and the social position she would have. Oh, he knew her kind. But this was too much. Mickie really liked Stephanie's daughter, but the woman was lonely and needy, imagining him as the answer to her problems. He didn't want to tell Stephanie exactly what he thought of her stunt or whom she had terrified, nor did he want to let her off scot-free. *Father, give me patience,* he thought. "I'll let Sarah know what happened and she'll come over and pick her up."

"Oh, that's not necessary. The girls are having a wonderful time. Why don't I just keep her until suppertime. You can stop by on your way home from work and have dinner with us…"

"Thank you, Stephanie," he said, "but I don't think that's possible. Sarah is the new housekeeper and she'll already have started supper. Besides, Mickie knows she's suppose to wait or call."

"Oh, I hope you're not going to chastise Mickie for the sitter's being late," Stephanie said in a pouty voice.

"No. No, not for that at all," he said, though he would have a talk with his daughter again about getting in a car with anyone other than the person supposed to pick her up. And walking home. He shuddered at the thought. "Look, I have to go. My housekeeper is on the other line. Thanks for calling." He hung up before she could get another word in.

"Sarah," he said into the other line, "she's two blocks over at Stephanie Williams's house."

Oh, thank you, Father, she whispered.

Justin was certain he could hear tears. "You might remember that next time you plan to pick Mickie up," he growled. He heard a swiftly indrawn breath but didn't care. He was still shaking himself. He tersely gave her directions to Stephanie Williams's house and hung up the phone.

"So, what has you looking so grim? Did you find a virus in our latest software package?" Bill quipped as he entered the office.

"Stephanie Williams just took my daughter home from school. It seems Mickie thought Sarah forgot to pick her up."

"And?"

"And?" Justin asked, staring incredulously at Bill.

"Well, for starters, I'm absolutely furious with Sarah. What are you shaking your head about?"

"I'd say you're feeling the aftereffects of terror."

Justin frowned. Bill was right. But he didn't have to like it. "Sarah has been here over a week. She should have been watching the time."

Bill raised an eyebrow.

"Mickie was about to walk home!" Justin exclaimed.

Bill chuckled. "I remember you telling me that Mickie once tried to walk to work to visit you."

Just like that, his fear and anger melted away. And with that, guilt swept in. He felt like a total heel for the way he'd treated Sarah on the phone a few minutes ago. Why hadn't he remembered this wasn't the first time his daughter had thought someone had forgotten to pick her up, after she'd waited only a few minutes? He knew it all came from the way Amy had left in the middle of the night, without saying goodbye to Mickie. The slightest incident triggered Mickie's feelings of abandonment, of being forgotten. Why had he been so angry at Sarah?

Yeah, Mickie had tried walking to his office, which was a forty-five-minute drive from his house. He shook his head and curved his lips as he remembered how Mrs. Winters had called him, hysterical that she couldn't find Mickie at school. He'd been terrified, too, until the school cross guard came walking back to the building with Mickie. Luckily, Mickie had asked the cross guard for directions downtown, explaining she had wanted to see her daddy. He shuddered recalling the long talk he'd had with his daughter about waiting where she was told to wait and trying to solve problems herself.

That had been just after Amy died.

"Is Sarah safe or should I go rescue her?"

Justin glanced up at Bill. "What do you mean?"

"Well, that look is off your face, which means Mickie is safe and sound and so is Sarah, so I guess she'll still be safe when you get home," Bill said, ignoring Justin's question.

He slouched in the chair in front of Justin. "So how's it going on the home front?"

Justin leaned back in his chair and crossed his hands over his stomach. "Fine. Why?"

Bill grinned. "I know both of you and how you're usually at each other's throats. I just wondered."

Justin shrugged. "Sarah's different." He thought about how she'd had dinner ready each night, and went to extra lengths every day to have everything done. She was working herself harder than any other housekeeper he'd ever had. He'd never thought of her as the domestic type. He'd also noticed circles under her eyes. He didn't think she was resting well, though she always smiled and had a kind word for him or a sweet smile and a hug for Mickie.

"She's eaten up with guilt."

"What?" Justin regarded Bill, almost having forgotten he was there.

"Guilt. You know what that is. She doesn't think she's good enough for anything."

This was new to Justin. He sat up straighter. "What do you mean? She certainly hasn't acted like a cowed individual."

Bill sighed. "Guilt manifests itself in different ways, Justin. Just because she's not walking around with the 'woe is me' look Amy wore whenever she felt sorry for herself doesn't mean—"

"Let's leave Amy out of this."

Bill nodded. "I'm sorry, Justin. What I mean is, well—" he shrugged, averting his eyes to the window and staring out "—Sarah feels guilty about her boyfriend dumping her, I think. Add that to the way she keeps messing up every relationship she's involved in—"

"She hasn't messed up any relationships that I know of," Justin said, defending her.

"What would you call what happened between the two of you?"

Justin paused. "Well, one mistake, then. She shouldn't have tried to take my daughter from me. But that's water under the bridge. Why does she blame herself for the breakup with her fiancé? What happened?"

Bill shrugged. "All I can say is, it wasn't Sarah's fault."

Justin accepted Bill's vague answer and respected Bill's ability to keep a confidence. Maybe that was why so many of Bill's friends confided in him. Yet why did he bring it up if he wasn't going to tell him? Justin wondered, frustrated.

"Look, just be careful about hurting her. Like when you go home today to discuss that she forgot your daughter. She's already blaming herself for everything that has gone wrong in the past decade, as far as I can tell. Don't add to the load."

Justin was shocked. He'd never pictured Sarah as the sensitive type who would carry around extra baggage like that. He'd always thought of her as a "full steam ahead" type who did what she wanted and didn't really care about what she left in her wake. He remembered his curt words to her the first couple of days and wondered now if she really had been feeling guilty over everything between them these past years. Was that why she'd come to him?

"So, have you decided to date her?"

"Date?" Justin sputtered.

Bill grinned. "Yeah, as in 'let's go out and see a movie'?"

Justin shot Bill a frown. "Of course not. She's my sister-in-law."

"Hey, I just wondered. You look so different."

Did he look different? He'd enjoyed having Sarah in his house this last week. She was sweet, kind and fun to talk with. But he wasn't in the market for a wife. Especially if what Bill said was true. For he wasn't going to marry someone else who came to him out of guilt.

Deciding to change the subject, he looked Bill up and down. "So, how's life been treating you? Looks like you've gained a little weight since you married."

Bill's grin spread across his face and he locked his hands behind his head. "Ah, yes, the little woman keeps me well-fed."

Justin stood, straightened his coat and came around the desk. "I'd like to hear what your wife would say about being called 'little woman.' Come on. If we're going to lunch, we'd better get out of here. I have a meeting at two-thirty.''

Bill chuckled and crossed the office with Justin.

He watched Bill's smile, the ease in his walk, how relaxed he was. Bill had certainly mellowed since marrying. A deep part in Justin yearned for that same thing that Bill had.

Would he ever find it?

Sarah paced the living room.

Mickie was on the swing in the backyard. Dinner was ready. But Justin wasn't home.

She had blown it today.

She'd thought being a baby-sitter would be a piece of cake.

And then she'd blown it.

How could she have forgotten Mickie? Justin's words came back to her. *You might remember that next time you plan to pick Mickie up.* It wasn't so much the words as the tone. He blamed her, as he should. But it had hurt just the same. She cared for Mickie, too. She hadn't meant to forget Mickie.

It was just that she was tired. So very tired. She'd been trying so hard to be a good housekeeper and everything that Mickie needed. Justin didn't know it, but she'd been up nights studying books on parenting and child development, as well as some of the latest housekeeping and cooking tips she found in women's magazines.

She was beginning to wonder how women had time for anything else but housekeeping. She'd stripped the floors and rewaxed them. She'd shampooed the carpets. And the curtains…well, they'd said in one magazine that they should be taken down once a month to be cleaned to keep any problems with allergies out of the house. Then there were the meals.

Sarah was used to buying canned or frozen convenience foods, not fresh meats and vegetables. Her eating habits weren't very healthy. But she couldn't expect Mickie or Justin to eat like that. So she'd been doing her best to fix new innovative meals each night. And the meals she was fixing took anywhere from two to three hours each. Some she had to start right after Justin went to work because meats had to be marinated or set out to thaw.

Today she'd been trying to get all the ingredients mixed for the chocolate coconut cake Mickie wanted, before she had to leave to pick up the child from school. She'd just happened to glance up at the clock and see she should have been at school that very minute.

Had she been thinking, she would have called the school and asked them to tell Mickie she was on her way and for them to keep an eye on her.

But she hadn't been thinking. She'd simply run out the door in her haste to reach her niece.

"I'm home."

Sarah whirled toward the door to see Justin just entering. He looked handsome.

He always looked handsome. The tweed coat and jeans with cowboy boots were so Texan on him. Odd to think he was the head of such a large corporation yet he dressed like this. He was always full of surprises. "Mickie is out back."

"I see." Justin put his briefcase in the hall closet

after taking out a few papers first. He started toward the library.

"May I talk to you?"

He looked over his shoulder, surprised. "Sure. I wanted to talk to you anyway."

Dread filled her. If she only got fired she'd be lucky. She wondered if he could bring her up on charges for abandonment or something.

Justin went to his desk and placed the papers there, then turned and leaned against the surface. "You look nice today."

She was shocked. But glad. She'd put on a new peach-colored top with her jeans knowing the shade complemented her coloring. Her hair was swept back into a French braid, clasped with a peach ribbon. While dressing this morning, she'd hoped taking more care with her appearance would lift her spirits, make her feel more feminine.

That was stupid, because she knew, deep down inside, that she would never be feminine enough. After all, she couldn't have children.... "I wanted to talk about this afternoon," she said, blocking the painful thought from her mind.

"I figured you did," Justin replied, his features relaxed.

"Look, Justin, no matter what you think of me, I wanted to tell you I'm really, really sorry for what happened. I got carried away with cooking and just let the hours slip by."

"It's all right, Sarah. It's not entirely your fault. It's partly Amy's," he added quietly.

Sarah stared, confused. What did this have to do with Amy?

"I don't understand."

How could Justin be so forgiving about this? She'd imagined he'd been waiting all along for an excuse to fire her and she'd just provided him one.

"Sit down." He motioned to a chair.

Sarah reluctantly eased onto the edge.

"The night Amy left, Mickie was asleep. Of course, Amy didn't wake her up to say good-bye. How could she have known Mickie would never see her again?" He hesitated, then went on. "Anyway, Mickie has never really gotten over the feelings of abandonment caused by the way Amy left us. If someone is supposed to pick her up and they're even a few minutes late, she can't handle it." He explained. "I've been late to pick her up myself, due to traffic or whatever only to find she's gone off with a friend."

Justin shook his head. "So far, no harm has been done. We've had long talks about her actions and she always promises not to go off again unless it was a real emergency."

"A real emergency?"

"I explained that if it was a real emergency—and her ride didn't come for say, an hour—she could go to her teacher, or find a policeman. Or even walk by herself to her friend's house who lives across from the school."

"Ah..." Sarah said. "That explains it I guess, but it still doesn't excuse me for forgetting to pick her up."

Justin shook his head. "How about if I just say I think Mickie takes after her aunt?"

Sarah thought about that. Her heartbeat increased as she wondered exactly what he could mean. He loved

his daughter. Did that mean he saw something good in her, Sarah? "I'm not exactly sure how to take that."

"Take it easy, Sarah. What I'm trying to say is I don't eat baby-sitters for lunch over minor mistakes."

"This wasn't minor."

"Yes, it was. Stephanie picked up Mickie from school, probably with some persuasion from Mickie," he added darkly. "I'll have a talk with Mickie again about waiting and taking rides from strangers. I'm sure you'll never forget her again, but if you are a little late, call the school."

She nodded. And trust God to keep Mickie safe. Boy, had she prayed while searching for Mickie and God had once again answered prayers by keeping her safe. "I'll finish dinner and get it on the table," she said, backing toward the door. "Thanks."

Justin nodded.

She couldn't understand why Justin had been so calm. She'd just known he was going to fire her and she'd once again lose the chance at the only family she would ever have. Longingly, she touched her stomach. For a moment a deep regret at what she couldn't have touched her soul. But then she was able to thank God. Because of that minor affliction she had woken up to what she already possessed and had neglected over the past two years. She had a wonderful niece and, she was beginning to see, an equally wonderful brother-in-law.

It would be enough. She had family, though she would never have her own family. She could surely forget that detail and go on with life, couldn't she?

Chapter Eight

Justin opened his eyes.

It was dark, the curtains pulled. Glancing at the bedside clock he saw it was two-thirty in the morning.

What had wakened him? Mickie hadn't crawled into bed with him. He listened but heard no noise in his room to account for the reason he'd awakened.

A whisper of noise reached him.

He sat up in bed, the crisp cotton sheet sliding down his chest. Listening again, he couldn't tell what it was he'd heard.

It hadn't come from downstairs. The alarm was on for the night and hadn't been triggered.

What could it have been? Maybe Mickie was having her nightmares again. She'd had nightmares right after Amy had died. But it had been at least six months since the last one.

He swung his long legs out of bed. After grabbing a sweatshirt and jeans from the end of the bed, he slipped them on.

He padded barefoot to the door, running a tired hand through his disheveled hair, then made his way down the hallway. He paused outside Mickie's door, then pushed it wide and peeked in to where he could see her silhouette form in bed. She lay still, curled up in a ball, one hand tucked under her chin, the other under the side of her face. She looked peaceful.

Frowning, he went over and tucked the sheet more securely about her. Had she gone back to sleep so quickly? he wondered.

He left Mickie's room. Just as he started down the hall, thinking he must have heard something downstairs such as the heating system, the sound came again. A whimpering moan, barely audible, sounding so forlorn that the hairs on the back of his neck stood up. Had he believed in ghosts, he would have thought the place haunted. But he didn't.

The sound emanated from somewhere he could now easily identify as he stood this close to Mickie's door in the hallway.

It was from Sarah's room.

He walked slowly over to her door. He listened and heard something—he wasn't sure what—then it was quiet. He tapped on the door.

"No, no, no!"

Her broken cries chilled him. No one could be in there. They would have run when he'd knocked. She had to be having a nightmare. "Sarah?" he called out.

She didn't answer.

He cracked open the door, just to check. Maybe her nightmare was over and he could sneak back to his room. But he knew that wasn't true the minute he saw his sister-in-law. She thrashed about in bed, heart-wrenching whimpers escaping her throat. What chilled him the most was the way she tried to hold them back, only allowing them to escape when she gasped for air.

"Sarah?" he said, louder, then glanced toward Mickie's room. He didn't want to wake the little girl. No telling how she would react if she saw Sarah like this.

He stepped into the room, pushed the door closed, then hurried to the edge of the bed. She was asleep on top of the covers, fully clothed. A book about child care lay open on the floor. It looked as if she'd fallen asleep reading tonight. "Sarah, honey, come on, wake up. It's okay."

She stilled for a moment, then thrashed again. "No, oh, no, please," she pleaded in a whisper.

He edged onto the side of the bed and raised a hand to her shoulder. Touching it, he shook her. "Come on, honey, wake up. It's okay."

The torment he saw on her face tore at his heart. Her eyes opened, but he wasn't sure if she was seeing him or not. Pain, excruciating and unbearable, filled her gaze.

"There're no babies. They're all just out of my reach."

Alarmed, he cupped her cheek. "Look at me, Sarah. You're dreaming." She stared at him and blinked. He could tell she'd finally woken up. "It's okay," he soothed her. "You were just dreaming. Something about the babies."

Her eyes slowly lost their unfocused quality and she gazed at him. "Babies?" she asked, then blinked again. She glanced around wildly before shuttering her gaze. "I don't know what you're talking about."

She was lying. He could see a bleakness, even a shame, in her eyes. What was going on here?

She shuddered from the aftereffects of the dream, he was sure, then she focused her vulnerable gaze on him again.

Maybe it was the abject look of need that made him notice her as a woman, but in that instant he did. He inhaled the perfumed scent of her soap and shampoo. Her skin was velvety soft where he cupped her cheek, her hair like silk. Had he ever noticed that before? Or had he noticed how the slope of her cheekbone and curve of her jaw made her look so feminine? And those eyes. Beautifully blue and so expressive. And staring at him just as intensely as he stared at her.

He cleared his throat, shocked at his attraction to her. Standing, he backed up. "I'm sorry for entering your room at night, Sarah. I promised you privacy. But you were having a bad dream. You had me worried."

He tried to smile but failed miserably.

She slid up in bed, pulling an afghan up to her armpits he noticed, even though she was fully dressed underneath. Great, she probably thought who knew what, waking up to find a man sitting on the edge of her bed. A dull flush crept up his cheeks. He was thankful for the darkness. He'd been married, had dated for years before that, and yet he'd never found himself in this situation.

"Sometimes, when I'm stressed out, my dreams can take an odd turn."

She still wasn't telling him the truth. He could tell

by the look in her lovely eyes. But right now, he thought accepting her words was the better part of valor. He didn't want to stay, knew it wasn't safe to stay because of his sudden urge to brush the stray strands of hair from her cheek, his impulse to comfort her, to persuade her to trust him.

"If you ever want to talk, I'd be happy to listen. I don't want you feeling *stressed out* over this job, Sarah. You're family."

Family. He had to remember that.

"Thank you, Justin, but I'm fine now."

"Well then." He retreated a couple of steps. "I'll just leave.

He backed into the wall, hooked the door with a finger and was gone before Sarah could say anything else.

Sarah watched him leave, the remnant of the dream fading and leaving her with only the longing she'd felt when she'd looked into Justin's eyes. Was she falling in love with him?

She couldn't feel that way about him. She just couldn't.

But she did.

She sighed and leaned back against the headboard. And when he'd seen the look in her eye, his distress had been obvious. It was apparent that he didn't share the same feelings she did. But it had simply been so easy to care for him. He was a good father, a good man from all she could tell. And yes, she admitted, he'd probably been a good man when she'd first met him, too. He had been trying to right what his partner had done.

But what was there to love about her? She had tried to take his child; she had most probably assisted in the problems in his marriage because she hadn't come to visit her sister. And now she had lost his child today. Not to mention that she had her own dark secret.

She remembered Stephanie Williams's scrutiny when she'd gone to get Mickie, the way the woman had studied her, then lifted a haughty eyebrow, as if she found Sarah wanting. It had angered Sarah just a bit, but also made her nervous. Stephanie evidently knew Justin well enough to feel free to pick up his child. Sarah had wondered if Stephanie might just have a right to be angry that Sarah had forgotten Mickie. Was Justin interested in Stephanie?

Still, she refused to rise to the bait and argue it with anyone but Justin. She might be wrong, but it was Justin's place to reprimand her, not some strange woman's.

Stiffening, she had gathered Mickie and her things and had come home.

She'd expected to be fired.

But she had received forgiveness, instead.

Something she had deserved termination for was not going to endear her to a man she'd already hurt. Still, he had forgiven her.

She shook her head in disbelief at where her thoughts were leading. Justin could never have feelings for her. He had loved Amy. He couldn't be interested in her. He certainly wouldn't be interested in her if he found out her secret, the secret she'd been dreaming about.

Tears filled her eyes. No, Justin was too good a

father not to want more children one day. He'd even told her so, that day they'd played with Mickie. So no matter how she felt, she knew those feelings would never be returned.

Sarah was just finishing up breakfast when Justin came in from running. She jumped when the back door opened.

He stopped short when he saw her. He looked great. Wearing gray jogging pants and a T-shirt that was now soaked with sweat, his hair in disarray from the wind, he still was handsome enough to make any woman take second notice. She hadn't been surprised when she'd first found out Justin ran. She'd guessed he exercised regularly to stay in such good shape.

"Sorry," he muttered. "I didn't mean to startle you."

"I just thought I was the first one up," she replied, pouring him a glass of juice. "I didn't realize you'd gone out already."

He nodded his thanks. "Mickie should be down soon." Nervously, he glanced at the wall clock. "I think she'll have something to say to you."

Sarah pushed at a stray piece of hair, feeling a smudge of flour on her face. She'd gotten out the cookbook, intent on making pancakes this morning for Justin and Mickie to try to make amends for the disaster yesterday. At his words, she paused in her actions. "Oh, Justin, you didn't yell at her over what happened, did you? I told you it was my fault."

Justin finished his juice, then placed the empty glass in the sink. "Let's just say I explained to Mickie that friend or not, she should never, ever get into someone else's car. I explained how it had scared both of us.''

Sarah relaxed. ''Oh.'' She turned her back on him and stirred the batter. ''That's fine. I just didn't want her to be in trouble for my mistake.''

She heard the squeak of his running shoes as he slowly crossed the floor. Tension crawled up her spine when she realized he was right behind her.

''I think we need to have a talk about this 'forgive and forget' thing.''

His words sent a shiver racing along her spine. She sensed his closeness, felt his concern for her, and his sensitivity to her feelings as well as Mickie's. She realized how much she would love to go on experiencing that every day.

''What do you mean?'' she asked, breathless. Her cheeks pinkened over her thoughts. She wanted to keep her back to him, afraid he might read the need of companionship in her eyes.

He wouldn't let her. He gently clasped her left shoulder and turned her until she faced him.

Her gaze rested on his chest. She couldn't look above that, until he put a hand under her chin and lifted it. When her eyes met his, she saw tenderness and understanding.

''You don't have to earn forgiveness, Sarah. Not for what happened yesterday or for what happened last night. Or even before that.''

''Nothing happened last night,'' she argued.

He smiled, a small tilting of the corners of his mouth that said he thought different. ''Stop trying to earn forgiveness and just accept your place here as family.''

''I'm the housekeeper,'' she whispered.

He smiled that smile again. ''You take care of the house, but you're more than just the housekeeper,'' he said, his brown eyes tenderly perusing her reaction to his words.

She tried not to show him any emotion, but with him holding her chin, it was impossible for him not to glean some hint of what she felt. She swallowed then nodded. ''Fine.''

His index finger stroked under her chin, then he released her and stepped back. ''Good.''

She thought she was off the hook when he headed for the living room. But he stopped just short of the room and spun back around. ''If you're not doing anything after breakfast, would you like to go to church with Mickie and me?''

Sarah stilled. He'd noticed she hadn't attended last week? She hadn't told him, or mentioned her reason. It was just so hard to go to the church that André's father went to and see him sitting there, looking through her as if she never existed.

She missed church dreadfully.

Maybe this was the opening of another door she should go through. She had intended to pull out a telephone book and start searching the directory after breakfast. But this would be so much better. She'd be going to a church where she knew at least two people. Granted, only one would be with her during the service, the very one who made her heart race every time he looked at her.

But wouldn't that be better than going into a church alone? And if she liked the church, then possibly her search for a new place would be over.

What would it hurt?

Coming to a decision, she turned to Justin and smiled at him. "I'd love to."

His eyes flared briefly. "Great. We leave here at nine-thirty to get there on time. I'll make sure Mickie is up and see you when breakfast is ready."

She nodded.

"Oh, and Sarah?"

She turned back. "Yes?"

"Just to give you a little extra time this morning, Mickie and I will load the dishwasher while you change."

"Oh, you don't—"

"Don't argue," he admonished. "We'll be down in a bit."

And he was gone, just like that, leaving Sarah standing alone in the kitchen. But the loneliness no longer bothered her. Sarah suddenly felt better than she had in months. She realized it was because she was looking forward to going to church with no worries over what she wore or how she looked. What an eye-opening revelation, she thought, stunned. She'd always felt pressured to dress for André's father. But Justin wouldn't care if her dress was simple or elegant, if she wore her hair in a French braid instead of a French twist. She had a feeling Justin was the type who enjoyed going to church simply to worship. And she was looking forward to that, indeed.

With a sense of freedom, she whispered another

small prayer. *Thank You, Father, that You led me here. I have a feeling I was in a bigger slump than I realized. Realizing how much I had dreaded going to church only goes to show me how out of line my priorities had gotten. Thank You for the joy You've restored and the forgiveness I saw in Justin's eyes. And most especially, Father, thank You that I'm once again going to be back in church with someone who evidently shares the excitement of going.*

She smiled and, with renewed energy, whipped the batter for her pancakes, thinking she'd better hurry or she'd end up making them all late.

Chapter Nine

She'd been right.

Justin took one glance at her simple drop-waist, floral dress and smiled. "You look great," he murmured, and held the door open for her as she climbed into the sleek Mercedes he'd been allowing her to drive.

He slid into the driver's seat. "Fasten your seat belt," he said to Mickie, glancing in the rearview mirror.

Sarah fastened her own, watching as Justin stretched to reach his belt and clasp it. In his charcoal gray suit, he, too, looked great. She had to grin over his tie, though.

"What has you smiling?"

She met his amused gaze. "Cartoon characters?" she asked, motioning to the brightly colored tie.

"I got to pick it out," Mickie said from the back seat. "I gave it to him for his birthday last year."

She tried not to laugh. "I see."

He lifted it and waved the end at Sarah, daring her

to say anything. "I think it's great," he said, grinning, his eyes twinkling. "Mickie has wonderful taste, don't you think?"

"Uh-huh. A great artistic eye."

She relaxed in the seat as Justin drove them to the service. When they got out of the car, Mickie ran ahead of them. Sarah started to call her back, but Justin forestalled her.

"Don't worry. This is a small church. Everyone knows everyone else. And the kids run in a gang until church starts."

Sure enough, two little boys and three other young girls met Mickie at the door, then in unison they turned and headed inside the church.

"The congregation of the church I went to numbered almost one thousand."

"I like the smaller church better. More intimate."

"Well, hello, Justin."

Sarah knew that voice—unfortunately. Turning, she saw she was right. Stephanie Williams, dressed in a fashionable, expensive-looking suit came forward. Her hair was perfectly styled in a sleek, chin-length cut and she brushed a stray lock aside with a flick of one manicured finger. Sarah looked down at her housework-chafed hands and felt positively dowdy.

She noticed Justin had a smile pasted on his face. But it was different from the smile she'd witnessed at home. It was what she thought of as his practiced business smile.

"Hello, Stephanie. You've met Sarah, haven't you?"

Stephanie ran her gaze over Sarah's dress and

hairdo, then turned back to Justin, dismissing her. "Why, yes, I have. Tell me, has Mickie gotten over her little trauma? The poor dear was inconsolable when I found her."

Sarah flushed but didn't comment.

"She's just fine," Justin replied.

"That's good," Stephanie cooed. "You'll have to come over someday soon for dinner, Justin. Bring Mickie. She always has so much fun with my daughter. I'm sure your housekeeper wouldn't mind a day off."

"My sister-in-law knows she can have a day off whenever she wants," Justin said.

Well, Sarah was thankful for that. She'd felt Stephanie's animosity and didn't understand it. But that line about coming over for dinner had made the woman's intentions perfectly clear. Stephanie had her eyes set on Justin.

"Oh, my, of course. I had forgotten she was your sister-in-law. Anyway, think about it. Maybe next Saturday or Sunday."

"We'll see," he said noncommittally. Then, dismissing Stephanie by turning to Sarah, he said, "We need to find a seat before the service starts. Have a nice day, Stephanie."

Taking Sarah's elbow, he led her off, leaving Stephanie standing in the foyer. Sarah raised an eyebrow. "Using me as a convenient excuse?"

"The woman is, ah, interested in getting better acquainted," he said.

"I hadn't noticed," Sarah remarked dryly.

"Go ahead, laugh. She's just about relentless.

Won't take no for an answer. Mickie said she insisted she get in the car and discouraged her from calling, saying she could phone when they got to her house."

Sarah frowned. "That's awful."

"Yeah, well, I told Mickie if that ever happened again to find the nearest teacher and hug her legs until she got her attention. She's not to go anywhere with anyone, no matter how insistent the person is. I told her the teacher would understand if she got out of line to tell her what was happening."

"How can you still talk to Stephanie after that?"

Justin shrugged. "I'm polite only because if I really said what I was feeling, I'd be at the altar praying for the next week or two. When I calm down enough to discuss it without saying anything in anger, I'll tell Stephanie not to try that again. I've already spoken to the principal. She assured me there would be no repeat performance. That's the important thing."

Sarah seated herself on the pew and watched as family after family came in, greeting others, laughing, talking, sharing what had happened during the week, before finally finding their seats. Several people stopped by and Justin introduced them to her. All were friendly, open and so kind. Justin was right. A small church was much nicer. Sarah had never attended a really small church of a hundred or so, which was what she estimated this group to be.

The music started and she stood. The songs were a lot like her old church's: upbeat, fast. Then the tempo slowed and became more worshipful, the songs talking about simple things—loving the Lord, praising Him for what He had done.

Peace flooded Sarah's soul as the congregation sang
and offered a special prayer for the sick and needy.
They mentioned a family who needed help with their
house. A recent storm had torn up one corner of the
roof and the pastor called for volunteers to help rebuild
it.

Then the pastor opened his Bible. "'Therefore,
there is no condemnation for those who are in Christ
Jesus because through Christ Jesus the law of the spirit
of life set me free from the law of sin and death.'
Romans 8:1.'' The pastor closed his Bible. "We're
going to discuss two things today in this sermon—sin,
which is the breaking of God's law and is forgiven
simply by asking God to forgive you for your trans-
gression, and guilt, which is after God has forgiven
you, the inability to forget it, as God does, but instead,
hold on to it in the form of guilt as your penance for
the wrong you've committed.''

Sarah sat up, her eyes widening. Oh, no, she
thought. This was a sermon she didn't want to hear,
one that was already convicting her.

"People don't often realize that conviction and guilt
are two different things. Whereas conviction brings
you to your knees to tell God you messed up and want
to start over again, guilt has you dropping your head
and hiding in shame over and over and over again.
Yet once it's forgiven it's forgotten.

"Self-condemnation brings it up again, not the spirit
of God. Jesus paid the price, and all we are required
to do is go to Him and confess our sins and He
is faithful and just to forgive us our sins. And forget them.

"When it includes others we've wronged, we should go to that person and apologize and ask for forgiveness. After that, though, it's off our shoulders. God doesn't require us to carry around unforgiveness against us, but simply to ask Him for forgiveness and any person we have wronged."

The preacher continued, but Sarah didn't hear. Her heart was too busy reacting to what the preacher had said. In all the time she'd been with Justin she realized she had been trying to earn his forgiveness because she hadn't let go of her guilt for what she'd done. Each time Justin had done something nice, said something sweet, she'd forced herself to work harder to prove how wrong she'd been. It had been like an arrow through her heart whenever he had smiled at her. The smiles, the attraction she felt, had only heaped guilt upon that condemnation. And now the pastor was explaining that once forgiven it should be forgotten.

Of course she realized that.

But she hadn't realized just what she'd been carrying around until the pastor had stated it so bluntly. She didn't know how long she sat there, stunned by how heavy a load lay on her shoulders, until Justin was standing next to her.

They had prayer and the pastor asked for those under a heavy burden to come down.

She went. When she bowed her head to pray, she was surprised to find Justin standing next to her and to feel his hand on her shoulder. Then she felt others around her who had come down for prayer, too.

Sarah prayed, admitting to God that she had been carrying around burdens that He had died for and would willingly take from her. She promised God she'd try harder not to hold on to the guilt and the past and to look to the future, instead.

When she was done, she felt lighter, freer than she had in a long time. They went back to their seats, gathered their Bibles and her purse and they left.

Many stopped her to say hi and welcome, then Mickie was there and they were in the car, ready to go. On the way home, Justin finally spoke.

"You look more relaxed than I've seen you since you came to work, Sarah."

She smiled. "I guess I am. You know, it's hard sometimes to forget the past and let go."

Justin laughed. "Don't I know. There are many things I regret about…" he said, glancing in the mirror at Mickie.

Sarah understood he was talking about Amy but didn't want to mention her name and alert his daughter. "But I finally received peace over those problems and had to just put them to rest. A few old ghosts are still hanging around, but you just have to put the past in the past and let it go."

This morning Sarah had done that with most of the things that had bothered her. But there was one thing she couldn't come to grips with, and that was her infertility. She'd lost André over it. There was nothing she could do about her condition, but she still felt guilty that she'd hurt André, no matter how rotten he'd treated her. But more than condemnation or guilt, she felt fear. She wondered how she would deal with telling anyone about her problem. "So let's say you had information that was going to hurt someone, should you feel guilty keeping that information secret?''

Justin chuckled. ''That's a hard one. Some people say to be honest no matter what. Others say a white lie is acceptable to spare feelings.'' His smile left as he thought about it. ''I suppose my feelings on the subject are that there should never be any secrets between a husband and a wife. Secrets break down the marriage, whereas the truth might hurt, but you can work through the hurt if you know there's a problem. As for others, what's not their business is just that, none of their business. If you don't like someone's dress you don't have to say, 'I love your dress' if you can say, instead, 'I love your hair.'''

She was relieved he felt that way. Because despite the wonderful service and the guilt she'd released over Amy's death and her treatment of this wonderful man, she still felt guilty for not telling him about what had truly prompted her to come to him in the first place: her infertility.

She knew it was because of her inability to have children that she'd suddenly started to consider family. Thinking of how much she was going to miss by never giving birth to children of her own had led her to pray. During that time with God, she realized she had wronged Justin and wanted to apologize. She'd hoped that if she apologized, then maybe he'd allow her to get to know her niece. She'd have a second chance at being a part of a family.

Justin's words—that some matters weren't anyone's business but a spouse's—encouraged her. She didn't feel as guilty over not telling him now and could relax.

After all, they weren't married. They certainly weren't involved. Why, he'd never asked her out on a date or anything.

So, what did she have to feel guilty about? Yes, life was indeed much better without the guilt and fears.

Chapter Ten

"You're asking me out on a date?"

Justin actually flushed. Then he got defensive. Oh, he didn't really show it, except the way his gaze turned colder and his body stiffened. Smiling that *business* smile of his, he said, "I need a dinner companion for a work-related meeting. I thought you would enjoy the night out, and since you haven't taken a day off since I hired you, I thought it my duty to drag you to a movie after. Of course, if you don't want to go to a movie, I certainly won't force you."

He wasn't fooling her. Justin never did anything without a reason. But he had to have some other reason to take her to a movie besides just wanting to be with her. She couldn't let herself believe he actually cared about her in that way. "What about Mickie?" she asked weakly, still in shock over his earlier query.

"My secretary has volunteered to watch Mickie. I gave her some money to rent some children's movies, plus pizza and popcorn. She'll bring her granddaughter, too, so Mickie will have someone to play with.''

The shock wore off, to be replaced with delight. It had been aeons since she'd gone to a movie. She couldn't even remember the last time. André had preferred supper theater or the country club. Realizing her thoughts, she forced down her excitement. She was actually trembling inside. There was no reason at all she should be so jittery. He needed her. It was that simple. And to pay her back for going with him to dinner, he was taking her to a movie.

Yes, that had to be it.

Still, the idea of a night out appealed to her. "That sounds fine," she said, hoping her voice was normal. "What time do you want me to be ready?"

"Five-thirty? I'll be home early to pick you up."

She nodded. He went out the door. Mickie was off school today because of teachers' meetings, so she was upstairs playing with a friend. Sarah set about straightening up. She felt so much more at ease with Justin since the Sunday service. She'd even thrown away all the magazines that had articles on keeping a perfect house.

Surveying the room, she noted the kitchen floor needed mopping and the living room needed to be picked up and vacuumed. She had two loads of laundry—mostly Mickie's—that needed washing.

Which meant she had plenty of time to bake Mickie her special chocolate coconut cake for tonight. The last time she'd tried, she'd been interrupted and then so upset by Mickie's disappearance that she'd never finished making it.

The day passed quickly as Sarah mopped the floor, fixed lunch, helped Mickie with her homework later that afternoon and got the laundry done before she felt ready to tackle the cake.

"Whatcha doing?"

Sarah glanced up from where she was pulling ingredients out of a cabinet. "I'm getting ready to make you a special treat for tonight." She gathered the flour, sugar and eggs. "I thought you were doing your math homework?"

Mickie smiled, twirling her hair with a finger. "I finished it." Suddenly, she stopped twirling her hair and looked up sweetly at Sarah. "I want to be a boo-tish-un," she said, frowning hard over the word.

Sarah grinned. "Beautician?" she asked.

"Yeah, boo-tish-un." She curled her fingers in her hair. "Do you have lipstick and stuff like that?"

Sarah poured the dry ingredients into a bowl. "I certainly do. Haven't you ever seen me sitting at the vanity when I put it on?"

Mickie shook her head. Frowning, she curled one of her long curls around her finger and held it above her eyes. "You have bangs and so does my friend, Katie. How come I don't have bangs?"

Sarah stopped stirring the cake mix. "Well, I suppose it's because your daddy never took you to get your hair cut."

"Could I have bangs?"

Sarah reached over and patted Mickie's head. "I imagine you can do whatever you want to your hair. Your daddy only wants you happy."

"Would your boo-tish-un give me bangs?" Mickie asked.

Sarah chuckled. "I'm afraid I cut my own bangs, Mickie. But we can talk to your daddy later, if you want, about getting your bangs cut."

She'd sloshed some cake batter over the side and she turned to clean it up. When she turned back, Mickie was pushing a chair over to watch her. Deciding to broach the subject of tonight, she asked Mickie. "You know your daddy's secretary is going to watch you this evening. She'll be bringing her granddaughter."

Mickie cut her eyes toward Sarah as she nonchalantly stuck her finger in the bowl and gathered up a lick of batter. "Miss Christine is nice, but I really like Shelley. She plays dolls, too."

"Well, I have it on good authority that Miss Christine is going to rent a movie and bring over pizza."

Mickie sucked her finger a moment longer before wiping it on her shirt. She grinned. "Pizza is almost my favorite food. Next to peanut butter and jelly. That's so cool."

Sarah grinned at how grown up Mickie tried to sound saying that.

Mickie turned around and sat down in the chair. She kicked her feet as she began to wind her hair around her finger. "Do you think Daddy would mind if I had bangs?"

Sarah wondered where the preoccupation with bangs had come from. "Not at all," she reassured her, and vowed to talk to Justin tonight about his daughter's desire. "Why don't you go find a board game to play. I'll finish up this cake, then meet you in your bedroom to play.''

Mickie nodded, slipped off the chair and walked out the door, never looking back, her fingers still curling and uncurling her hair.

As Sarah finished the cake, she wondered what she was going to wear tonight. She'd unpacked a few things from storage. The only nice outfit she had was still in a box. It was black and had a scooped neck and capped sleeves. Formfitting, it stopped just above the knees. She'd worn it whenever she'd gone to the theater with André. It was worth a try. Of course, she had a blue two-piece outfit that was nice, but she thought that maybe the black would be more formal.

She decided to go ahead and wear the blue outfit. It had a short straight skirt, white knit top and a blue sweater-style jacket. She wore it for business sometimes, but with the jacket off, it would look casual at the movie. No reason to break out the black thing when she'd always hated that dress.

She slipped the cake in the oven, happy she was finally getting to bake it for Mickie. Then she hurried out to the garage to find the blue outfit. She had some great handmade silver jewelry that would be fun to wear with it. She'd worn the earrings and bracelets when she'd started working at Watson and Watson but had stopped when André's father had frowned at her appearance. The jewelry didn't look businesslike, he'd said.

Quickly, she hunted the jewelry out, then carried it to her room with her outfit. But when she unpacked the outfit, it looked totally wrinkled. ''I need to iron something real quick, Mickie, then we'll have that game,'' she called, heading back downstairs with her clothes.

She couldn't believe Mickie had allowed her this much time without interrupting. Usually, Mickie came down every five minutes or so to ask her a question.

Sarah looked at her watch. She had enough time to iron, go upstairs, play a game with Mickie until the cake was done, then shower and dress and be ready before Justin got home.

She pulled out the iron, then ran it lightly over her skirt and top. As she ironed, she wondered why Mickie hadn't impatiently come to find her.

After quickly finishing, she put the iron away, then went upstairs. ''Mickie?'' she called, uneasy at how quiet it was.

She checked in each room. ''Mickie?'' she called again, her unease growing to panic. Had Mickie run away? Surely after the talk her dad had given her, she wouldn't go anywhere again on her own. ''Mickie?'' she said, louder, checking under her bed and out the window.

Then she heard it.

A muffled sound coming from the closet.

Concern replaced fear and she hurried over to the door. ''Mickie, honey,'' she called, opening the door.

The little girl was at the back of the closet, amid the shoes and boxes. Her head was bowed over her arms, which were propped on her knees. And her shoulders shook. Sarah knelt in front of her, totally mystified. ''Mickie, honey, what is it?''

"Um, I, uh, was playing boo-tish-un," she mumbled.

Sarah reached out, but hesitated to touch her. Mickie might really want to be alone right now. "Can you say that again, Mickie?" she asked, thinking that if she could understand her, then maybe she'd know how to handle the situation.

"Daddy's gonna be mad."

What did Justin have to do with this? Then it dawned on Sarah. Justin was the law of the house in his little girl's eyes. Sarah had done something wrong. "Oh, Sarah, honey, if you've done something wrong, your daddy's not going to get mad, unless you endangered your life. Tell me what happened."

Still the little girl wouldn't look up. "I wanted to be beautiful like you. I don't remember how Mama looked. But I bet she had bangs, too. She doesn't have any hair in my picture."

Sarah knew the only picture of Amy that Mickie had was in Mickie's room. Amy had her hair slicked back in a tight professional-looking bun in the photo. No, Amy had never had bangs.

A feeling of dread suddenly coiled in the pit of Sarah's stomach. "Mickie, look up at me, dear. Did you cut your hair?"

The little girl started sobbing again. "It's awful. I'll never be a boo-tish-un."

"Look at me, Mickie."

Sarah waited. Finally, Mickie lifted her head. *Oh, Father, Justin is going to be mad over this. Help me to handle the situation.*

Mickie's hair was cut in a slash across the front of

her head. One eye was completely covered, and in a couple of spots her hair stuck out awkwardly on top, which told Sarah bangs weren't the only thing that had suffered Mickie's attempts.

"Where'd you find the makeup?" Sarah asked gently. Mauve lipstick—if Sarah wasn't mistaken it was her lipstick—covered the girl's mouth and blush was on her cheeks. Brown eye shadow was under both eyes and even spotted her forehead. Looking at Mickie's hands, Sarah saw smears and realized the little girl had been wiping away tears. "Don't answer that. I take it you found my makeup, in the location I volunteered earlier."

She reached for Mickie's hand and pulled her out of the closet. "Come on, sweetie, let's go get you cleaned up, then we'll put some makeup on you and fix your hair nicely for your daddy."

"It can't be fixed," the little girl cried.

"Of course it can," Sarah soothed. "And next week I promise to take you to a beautician if you still want to go, and let her explain about cutting hair."

She escorted the little girl into the bathroom. "We'll use my special cleaner to get all this off. It's creamy and cool and won't hurt the way scrubbing with a washcloth does," she teased.

And she proceeded to remove every speck of makeup from Mickie's face.

"Now for the hair. Stick your head under the faucet."

Mickie did.

Sarah ran her hands through the mounds and mounds of curly hair. "Has your daddy ever cut it?"

"No," Mickie sniffled, though she sounded much better than she had only minutes before. "He said Mama never would cut it."

Oh, boy, she thought. When she was done wetting Mickie's hair, Sarah ran a towel over it, then combed it. Well, she decided, looking at the mess, she'd started this, she might as well go ahead and finish it. "Do you want it medium length like mine or do you want to keep it long like your mommy's?" she questioned, thinking Mickie would, of course, pick the latter.

"Like yours," Mickie immediately replied.

Of course. She should have known. "Let's tackle those bangs first," she said, then with a deep breath she combed the hair over the child's face.

Finding the shortest piece, which was, luckily, not too awfully short, she began snipping. "Why, look at that," Sarah exclaimed, "you're losing all your curl!"

The curly ends disappeared and only a small wave remained. She quickly feathered the hair around the child's face, then worked painstakingly to layer it where the little girl had left it awkward.

Mickie's eyes widened. "Why don't I have no more curl?"

"You know, your mommy's hair did the same thing when she was a little girl. I'd forgotten that. She kept just a bit of wave, but all the curl disappeared. Maybe that's why your mom never wanted to cut your hair."

Sarah lifted and snipped and combed and snipped some more, until she had a towelful of leftovers. "I think you have more hair down there than you do up here," she said, tapping Mickie's head on the last word.

"I'm beautiful," Mickie said, her eyes shining.

"Oh, honey," Sarah said, turning her around and hugging her, "you've always been beautiful. But there's something more than outward beauty and that's what's in your heart. As long as you are good in there, that's all that matters." She kissed her. "Come on. Let's put a little makeup on to complete the rest."

Mickie frowned.

"Hey, trust me." She led Mickie from her bathroom to her vanity. After she sat her down, she took out a compact of powder. "Now, little girls have to wear only certain types of makeup. You'll find that as you get older you have to keep changing the type of makeup you wear. This is the best type. It's young girls' makeup. As a matter of fact, even though I'm getting old, I can still wear this."

She took the pad and rubbed it over the powder. "Let's dust your face with this. See how you bring it down your nose and over your cheeks and on your forehead? We only want a bit. We don't want to look fake."

"Like Miss Stephanie?"

Although Mickie had asked the question innocently, Sarah couldn't resist smiling. "Well, some women like to wear more makeup. But I myself think makeup should cover only the freckles on my nose and stuff like that." She put down the compact and met Mickie's eyes in the mirror.

"As for lipstick, the color you had on was way too dark. However, I just happen to have something I wear on my lips when I'm outside."

She pulled out a cherry-flavored conditioner for

chapped lips. "It's almost like lipstick and even tastes good. Pucker up."

Mickie did, wrinkling her nose. "Daddy says this is my face when I eat a lemon."

Sarah laughed and applied the lipstick. "Oh, that's perfect!"

Mickie looked around and grinned. "I like it. But Daddy will tell me I shouldn't wear makeup."

"I bet he doesn't mind this." In actuality, Sarah couldn't see Mickie's powder, and it looked as though she'd licked her lips.

Mickie grinned. "I can't wait to show Daddy when he gets home."

When he gets home? Oh, dear! Sarah glanced at her watch. She'd been up here an hour and a half.

Mickie sniffed. "What's that?"

Sarah smelled it at the same time. "The cake!"

She'd completely forgotten about the cake. "It's burning!"

Sarah turned to run downstairs. As if sensing her anxiety, the fire alarms chose that moment to go off. Shrieks filled the air as the smoke began to drift up the stairs. "Mickie, run outside! I'll go check and make sure nothing is really on fire."

She took off down the hall, Mickie's hand in hers. She had really messed things up this time. Justin was due home any minute and his house was likely on fire. Justin would surely dismiss her this time.

Chapter Eleven

Justin had just reached for his briefcase, when he heard the smoke alarms. He jerked his head toward the house and his heart exploded in his chest. Forgetting the briefcase, he took off across the garage and burst in through the kitchen door, right into swirling smoke.

He immediately realized it was coming from the oven. "Sarah!" he called, dashing over and jerking the stove door open, only to fall back coughing as black smoke came pouring out.

After grabbing the oven mittens, he reached in and pulled out a pan. He heard the swinging door that led to the kitchen slam against the wall; heard a gasp and realized Sarah had arrived. "Where's Mickie?" he demanded, dropping the black thing in the round cake pan into the sink.

"She's outside. I told her to wait out there until I knew what was going on."

The blaring alarm was so strident he could hardly

hear her. She was squinting, holding her hands over her ears, coughing each time she tried to take a breath, tears streaming down her face.

He turned on the water, and a loud hissing issued from the lump.

"I'm sorry," she said.

"What?" he asked, then shook his head and pushed past her. He grabbed a kitchen chair, dragged it over beside the wall and stood on it. Once he'd pulled the smoke alarm off the wall, he jerked out the battery.

The cessation of noise was so absolute the silence was almost as painful as the earlier din. Justin returned to the sink and simply stared at her, still gripping the hot pads in his hands.

She couldn't tell by his face if he was mad or not. "I was making a cake."

"You burned it." He said it simply, no inflection in his voice to hint at how angry he might be.

"I can explain," she began.

He turned from her and shut off the water. Staring at the hard black lump in the pan, he finally said, "That was a cake?"

"Chocolate coconut," she confirmed.

He pushed open the window over the sink. The garage door was still open and the fan overhead was running.

"Do you want to hear my explanation now?"

"Daddy's home!" Mickie came running into the house through the garage door.

Before she could say a word, Justin turned to greet his daughter—and froze. "Mickie?" His voice rose on the last syllable.

Mickie threw herself at her daddy's legs. "Don't I look beautiful?" she said, and gave him a hug.

He frowned at Sarah. "Yes, sweetheart, you look absolutely fabulous. You're my special little darling. Now, what are you doing in the house when the fire alarm is going off?"

"You're home and the alarm stopped." Mickie smiled up innocently at her daddy. "I wanted to see if Aunt Sarah had messed up the cake again."

"Thanks a lot, kiddo," Sarah muttered.

"It looks that way," Justin added.

Mickie sighed. "I guess after pizza I can have peanut butter and jelly for dessert."

Justin chuckled. "Sounds fine. You wanna run out back and play on the swing? I'd like to talk to your aunt Sarah while we clean this up. Besides, it's still sorta smelly in here, isn't it?" He wrinkled his nose as if smelling something really disgusting.

Mickie giggled. "You're silly, Daddy."

She skipped out the door and Sarah watched as she unlatched the gate and went into the backyard.

When she was gone, Justin turned back to Sarah. His smile was gone and his eyes were serious. "Care to explain what happened?"

She grimaced. "I did offer."

He tossed down the hot mitts and motioned her into the living room. After divesting himself of his suit jacket, he tossed it over the back of the couch and sank down. "Go on."

"Mickie decided that she wants to be a beautician."

"And?" he questioned when she hesitated.

"Well, I was making a cake—"

"I gathered that," he remarked dryly.

"And," she said, shooting him a dark look, "well, I didn't realize that Mickie might take it into her head to start practicing her salon skills immediately."

She settled on a chair, the adrenaline rush leaving her suddenly shaky. "I straightened it up as best I could, but that meant a lot of cutting. I'm sorry if it doesn't look good. I'm really sorry about the cake, too. I just got so involved with her..." She trailed off and shrugged.

"At least my house is still standing," he replied.

Sarah sighed and stood. "I have to clean the bathroom upstairs, then I guess I'll retire to my room for the night. I'm really sorry about all the trouble."

Justin sat up, alarm in his eyes as his gaze connected with hers. "Retire? Have you forgotten your promise to go out with me tonight?"

Sarah paused, but she kept her gaze steady as she replied, "After the mess I've made and the mess I'll have to leave the house in if I attend, you still want me to go?"

He shrugged, then leaned back in the chair looking nonchalant, as if she hadn't just caused a major disaster. "Accidents happen. And the housework will be here in the morning. Besides, Mickie is excited about the pizza. She doesn't need the cake tonight."

Sarah couldn't believe he still wanted her to go out with him. She smiled with relief. "Give me a few minutes to get ready."

Justin watched her rush up the stairs and chuckled over her sudden energy. His heart was still beating a staccato over the fire alarm. All he could picture when he'd heard the blaring noise was Mickie and Sarah burning in the house before he could get to them. It had shaken him and awoken him to just how he felt about Sarah. In the past few weeks she'd become a part of his life, for better and worse.

Despite her forgetting to pick up Mickie and the other minor mishaps, things were working out well. At least, they had been until that fire alarm today. Talk about an eye-opening experience. He realized how much he'd come to enjoy having Sarah around. She was wonderful, fun, not at all the way she had been when he'd known her before Amy's death. She was also tender and caring, as Mickie's haircut attested.

Justin had been uncomfortable about taking Mickie to a salon for a haircut. Amy had always talked about letting Mickie's hair grow until she was old enough to decide for herself how she wanted it styled. She had insisted the child would want curly hair when she was older. Evidently, he hadn't realized Mickie had wanted to experience what her other friends had—a simple haircut. Or maybe she'd just wanted it to be short like Sarah's. Who knows? But one thing was certain—when Mickie had messed up her hair, Sarah had taken time with her to fix it in a very pretty style and had somehow made Mickie feel beautiful all at once.

She was good for Mickie. And Mickie was falling under her spell. Several nights he'd heard Sarah reading to Mickie before he got up there to tuck Mickie in. And they'd shared secret smiles occasionally—girl smiles, he called them.

And here he was taking Sarah out on a date tonight. How had his feelings become involved? He had promised himself not to fall for a woman who couldn't love him back. He had insisted his odd feelings for Sarah were crazy and nothing could come of it. But now he discovered he already cared deeply for Sarah. He wasn't sure if it was love or not, but knew it could easily develop into that. His feelings today were a dead giveaway. When he'd heard the alarm, his first thought after Mickie was what would he do without Sarah?

He sighed. *Is it possible, Father, that she could actually come to love me one day? Could she forget it was her sister I married and her sister I made so unhappy that she ended up dying on a rainy highway? After all, she did come to apologize for trying to take Mickie away and says she shares the blame for the problems with Amy.*

Could she eventually come to love him?

There was only one way to find out. Things were going in a much different direction than he'd planned. So he would let things develop, ask Sarah out when he could, let her get to know him and spend time getting to know her. If it was God's will that she be his soul mate for the rest of his life, God would work things out between them. *I put it in your hands, Heavenly Father.*

He glanced at his watch and realized he needed to change if he was going to be downstairs and presentable when Christine got here with her granddaughter and he and Sarah were going to make it to the dinner engagement on time.

Hurrying up the stairs, he wondered just what their dinner was going to be like.

* * *

"Your meeting is at Jon Bilovi's?" Sarah asked, staring in surprise at the really nice restaurant. "I'd have worn something else if I'd known we were coming here."

Justin smiled, his gaze taking in her outfit. "Oh, no, Sarah. How could you say that? You're a knockout in that."

Sarah's hand went to the soft bun on her head—a nervous gesture to cover Justin's comment. What had he meant by that? Did he really like it? Was he just flirting with her? No, he wouldn't flirt. Of course not. It was just what a man said to a woman, though the look in his eyes made her nervous. He didn't find her attractive, did he?

He came around and opened her door. "Relax, sweetheart. Not meaning to hurt you," he said, shutting the door behind her and slipping his hand to the small of her back, "but you were engaged not too long ago. Surely you know how to take a compliment."

"Of course I do," she muttered. But André had never looked at her quite the way Justin had. That was what bothered her. Justin hadn't looked at her like *that* before, either. What was going on here?

"Who are we meeting?" she asked as they walked into the darkened restaurant and Justin escorted her to one of the back rooms.

"Phillip, my assistant, and his fiancée, Julie. He's tall, blond and has a megawatt smile. You'll like him. He's easy to get along with—as long as he's not involved in a business deal. And one of the lawyers we've just taken on to help with different things that need doing will be there. He'll also act as an adviser about certain laws in this state. His name is Drydan Watson and his wife, Barbara, should be with him.''

Sarah stiffened, but Justin didn't notice, as he had removed his hand from her back and was stretching it out toward the very man who had caused Sarah's reaction.

Drydan Watson, her ex-boss and father of her ex-fiancé, sat at the table in the private dining room they'd just entered.

Sarah felt nauseous, thought about running away, then firmed her spine. *Father, please help me get through this,* she prayed. Pasting a smile on her face, she continued forward.

She noted the welcoming smiles on Phillip's and Julie's faces. Not so Drydan or his wife, Barbara, who turned her head to study a picture.

''And this is Sarah Connelly,'' Justin was saying as he pulled out the chair directly across from Drydan, ''my sister-in-law.''

Julie smiled and Phillip stood and shook her hand. Turning her smile upon Drydan, she said, ''We've met,'' and seated herself.

An odd look flashed in Justin's eyes, then was gone as he took his seat at the head of the table.

''So, Drydan,'' Justin said, leaning forward and picking up his menu, ''tell me what you think of the latest merger prospect of East Texas Software.''

Drydan launched into his opinion and Sarah relaxed. As long as Justin kept him speaking, she could handle the situation. Barbara refused to look at her and Julie was making small talk.

Feeling a gaze on her, she glanced up to find Drydan staring right at her as Phillip snagged Justin's attention. She was shocked at the anger in his eyes.

Sarah realized Drydan was doing his best to make her uncomfortable.

And he was succeeding. Should she get up and leave? But that would hurt Justin. Perhaps just a short trip to the bathroom. But then Drydan might think her a coward.

With a sigh of resignation, she realized she would just have to put up with him. She didn't want to be here, though. After all, he was the one who had always thought her beneath his family. He and Barbara, that is, she added as she saw the way Barbara had drawn Julie's attention away from her.

The food came shortly, with conversation flowing easily around her. Justin had engaged her a few times in conversation, but after her monosyllabic answers, he stopped trying. She did make an effort to smile at him and reassure him she wasn't angry. She could feel the tension coming off him in waves. What could she say to Justin in front of these people?

She choked down every bite of food into a stomach that felt as though it was tied up in knots, and barely finished a third of her meal.

When Justin pushed back his chair, she knew she couldn't say polite goodbyes to these people. Her pain was too fresh. Besides, if she uttered one word to Drydan, she was certain he would reply something to embarrass her. He hadn't stopped shooting her looks all night.

"Excuse me, Justin," she said as he pulled her chair out. "I'll meet you out front."

Again he gave her that odd, piercing stare, then he nodded.

She escaped to the bathroom. As soon as the door was closed, she let her shoulders drop. André's parents. What had they thought of her being there with Justin tonight? Why would Justin associate with someone like them?

Of course, Drydan was a pretty good lawyer; he even went to church. But he certainly didn't practice what was preached. She'd always thought him a little intimidating. His wife was condescending while acting helpful. But André hadn't been like them. At least, she'd thought that. It was awful to find out she and Drydan were both working for the same man.

A shudder rippled through her.

At least she wouldn't have to see much of him, unless Justin invited him over for dinner.

After washing her hands, she quickly dried them, checked her hair and lipstick, then finally headed out the door. Justin would be waiting, and surely Drydan and his wife would be gone by now.

Drydan stood by the phones, talking into one, but the minute he saw her, he hung up.

"It sure didn't take you long, did it?"

Sarah braced herself. "I'm sorry you're bitter about my breakup with your son, but I have nothing to say, Mr. Watson," she said, trying to get around him. His large frame blocked her exit.

"I told André I had you pegged from the beginning. Jumping from one man to another, just as I said—another fortune hunter."

The blood drained from her face at his harsh and untrue words.

But Drydan wasn't done. "Does Justin know your little secret? Would he be so interested then, I wonder, if he found out?"

Infertile. He would tell Justin she was infertile just out of spite. The world spun and she thought she would have to rush right back into the bathroom and be sick. Then she realized something. "You won't tell him. It'd be too embarrassing for him to find out André had actually broken our engagement because he found out I was flawed."

She saw she'd scored a point.

Squaring her shoulders, she advanced. "And it wouldn't matter if you did, Mr. Watson. Justin is my brother-in-law and a good Christian man. I'm his housekeeper and sitter. There's no romantic relationship between us, so that wouldn't matter."

She strode past him through the space that had opened up when he'd stepped back in anger.

"Mark my words, missy. He won't have you. No man will when he finds out your secret."

She tuned out his voice and continued to the lobby. She was heading toward the door, when a touch on her arm stopped her. She jumped and whirled around.

"Sarah, are you okay?" Justin stood there, looking, for all the world, like a concerned date.

No man will have you. She swallowed and tried to smile. "I'm fine. I thought you'd be outside."

"I didn't want you going to the car alone. Besides, I have a couple of questions to ask you."

They walked out of the restaurant together. "Oh?"

she said, trying to sound carefree and failing miserably.

"The first is, do you still want to go to the movie?"

"Of course," she immediately replied.

"And the second,..." he paused as he got to the car. Unlocking the door, he opened it and stepped back to allow her to enter.

She waited, but he didn't go on. Nor did he close the door. Finally, she looked up at him. That was what he'd been waiting for.

"What's going on between you and Drydan?"

She knew she was going to be sick.

Chapter Twelve

"Please just drive."

Justin watched Sarah as she visibly shook while trying to remove her purse strap from her shoulder. Such
a simple task had become a major chore. He closed
her door and went around to his side of the car. After
sliding in, he started the car and drove off. He was
halfway to the movie before she finally asked, "Why
is Watson working for you?"

He shrugged. "Just one of the lawyers we hired to
help with the overflow. He has a very sound head on
his shoulders, has done wonders for other companies
and is known as a very good attorney with contracts
and such."

"Oh, he is. He's very good at what he does. Probably at the very top."

"How would you know that, Sarah?" But he had a
feeling he knew. He'd never really heard the last name
of her fiancé. Could it be—

"My ex-boss. I was engaged to his son."

Bingo.

"You see, he never liked me. Once André and I were serious, Drydan did everything in his power to get me to quit. He's the one who delivered the news that I was fired. And he enjoyed telling me a minute ago that I'd proven him true by chasing after you, hoping to cash in on your fortune."

"He said what!" The car swerved, but Justin immediately jerked the wheel, steering the vehicle back into his lane.

Sarah's eyes widened in shock as she stared at Justin. Her misery vanished as she realized Justin was absolutely furious. "I'm sorry, Justin. That's just Drydan. He doesn't like me and wanted to make sure he scored a few points. I didn't mean to cause any problems when I saw him by the phones. Maybe I should have just pleaded illness and left—"

"Not another word."

She snapped her mouth shut, taken aback by the savage sound of his voice.

"Don't apologize for things that aren't your fault. That's one pet peeve I have developed about you that's going to drive me crazy, Sarah. You take *too* much blame."

"You don't have to be mad at me!" she cried.

Justin shook his head, his anger cooling some. "I'm not mad at you. I'm angry at what I allowed to go on when I was only a few feet away. Why didn't you tell me, Sarah, that you were uncomfortable? I never would've stayed."

She shrugged. "It was a business meeting—"

"It could have taken place later."

"I didn't know that!" she argued, irritably.

"Point made," he said.

And she thought he actually grumbled the words. Turning, she saw he was frowning out the windshield. "Please, don't be angry," she said softly, sorry she had repeated what Drydan had told her.

Finally, he sighed. "I'll try. After all, I don't want you to think I'm *always* like this."

He actually gave her a small grin.

"I think I know that," she replied, smiling.

"Do you?" he asked quietly, intensely.

She didn't answer. She didn't have to because Justin returned his gaze to the street as they arrived at the movie theater.

After he parked, he came around and opened her door again. This time he reached in and took her hand. Shaking his head, he smacked his lips. "I think between the movie and you, that you, darlin', are going to be the better to watch."

She laughed. "What do you mean by that?"

"I'm taking you to one of those sappy romantic movies. I figured that's what all women would want to see." He gave her a long-suffering look.

"Actually," she replied, blithely lying, "I'm a horror person myself."

His eyes widened, then gleamed with amusement. "*Revenge of the Swamp Monster* is showing, if you prefer. I hear aliens came to Earth and repaired the creature so that he lives once again."

She burst out laughing and started across the parking lot with him. "I give in. Sappy, syrupy romance is fine."

While Sarah waited, Justin paid for two tickets. "It's been aeons since I've been to a movie theater," she confided as they went inside.

"Then I think you should enjoy first class," he replied, leading her over to the concessions.

"Oh, please, don't buy those. The prices at these counters are outrageous."

"You didn't eat any dinner. I don't want to sit through the entire show listening to your stomach growl."

She flushed.

He chuckled. "A 'monster buster popcorn,'" he said, reading from the menu, "and two medium drinks."

"You don't expect to eat all that popcorn, do you?" Sarah asked, aghast at the size of the popcorn he'd ordered.

"If we don't I can guarantee you that Mickie will finish off the leftovers. She eats about half of one of these whenever we come to the movies. She loves popcorn."

"As much as peanut butter and jelly?"

"I don't think so." He grinned. "Of course, you have to understand, in six months or so she'll have another all-time-favorite food."

They found seats just in time—the lights were already dimming. Sarah had never realized how close the seats were before. Justin's arm brushed hers as he jerked on his jacket before finally getting it off. His light musky cologne wafted over to her and she inhaled it, enjoying the scent and the warmth of his presence next to her.

How could she have guessed he would have stood up for her against Drydan? Even André hadn't done that. André had only shrugged and said his father and mother were worried about him. He'd never been outraged or offended by the way his parents had insulted her. But Justin had. And he'd felt upset he hadn't been there to defend her. It gave her a very warm, special feeling to know he wasn't angry with her.

She turned her attention to the screen and began to eat popcorn. Occasionally, their hands would bump and she and Justin would each offer an "Excuse me." The tension—tension she was still surprised to find between them—built.

She was so nervous she missed the entire movie. All she caught was that it was about two people who fell in love, but the disclosure of some deep dark secret broke them apart. In the end, love overcame the obstacle.

The story line did nothing for her stretched nerves. There was no love between her and Justin. She felt only an attraction. He'd invited her out and let her feel like an adult for a night. However, the plot, along with Drydan's words, made her wonder how Justin would feel if he suddenly found out what had originally motivated her to pray and finally come see him.

Would he be hurt? Angry? Bitter?

It wasn't that she didn't care for him, that she hadn't wanted to see Mickie before she'd found out she was infertile. It was just that…what?

That her priorities hadn't been right? That she'd had so many things going in her life that she'd relegated Justin and Mickie to the far corners of her mind?

They were all awful reasons, but all true. How self-centered she could be? The occasional brush of his leg or arm was driving her crazy! she thought, distracted once again by the warm, intimate brush of his trousers against her nylon-covered leg.

"You ready?"

She blinked, glanced at Justin and realized the credits were just coming up on the screen. She nodded. "A good movie," she said.

"I should have chosen action." He chuckled, then winked. "I would've gotten more of a reaction from you."

She laughed, not sure what he meant. His warm hand slipped to her back and again she recognized how much of a gentleman Justin was.

He escorted her to the car and closed the door behind her before slipping in on his own side. The ride was quiet, not filled with chatter, as they drove along the highway.

"Did you really enjoy the movie?" he asked as they approached his house.

"Very much," Sarah murmured. "Or, at least, going out. I hadn't realized just how much my world had started revolving around Mickie and housework."

He chuckled again, a husky sound that sent shivers down her arms.

"I force myself to take off at least once a month and go to a museum during lunch or just for a walk. It not only gets me away from the office but gives me time to relax and think about what I have, how lucky I am. Just to enjoy being a person instead of a dad or a president of his own company."

"Well, I can say it was nice. I think I'd forgotten what quiet is. Or just sitting still."

He pulled into the driveway, right into the garage, and turned off the engine. The garage light automatically came on, illuminating the way to the kitchen door.

She pushed open her own door and slipped out of the car before he could come around.

"Shame on you," he chided, standing in front of the vehicle.

She shrugged. "You're tired."

He smiled, an odd smile. "Now, why would you say that?"

"You've been so quiet."

"I was just thinking," he replied, escorting her to the door.

His hand was at her back again, the light touch thoroughly distracting her.

Reaching into his pocket, he pulled out his keys—and promptly dropped them.

Sarah, nervous for some unknown reason, tried to get them at the same time he did. She chuckled self-consciously and stood back up, only to find she was inches from Justin. Her gaze snapped up to his.

Justin's eyes darkened as he looked at her face, her eyes and, finally, her mouth.

Frozen, Sarah watched as his head bent. Slowly, his mouth closed the distance to her lips.

Her breathing increased.

What in the world is happening? her mind screamed at her. *This is Justin!* But it didn't matter. She felt warm, strong hands on her arms, and then she was being pulled against Justin's hard frame. She relaxed in his embrace as she told herself no. Then she lifted her lips to his.

Warm, soft, tender. Those were the words to describe how it felt to be kissed by Justin Warner. His arms slid behind her and held her to him; his lips touched hers and caressed her tenderly, then with more urgency. She kissed him back, a tumult of warm, sweet emotions swirling within her.

Then Justin eased back. When she opened her eyes, he was staring at her in shock.

Her own breathing was unsteady. But she flushed at the surprised look on his face. "What? Have I grown two heads?" she quipped, but her voice came out like a croak, definitely not normal.

Justin didn't get the chance to answer, she was thankful, for Christine showed up at the door and pulled it open.

"I thought I heard you get home. Did you forget your key?"

Justin stepped back. Sarah immediately slipped around Christine. "Good night. Thanks," she called, and strode quickly toward the stairs.

Have I grown two heads? Great line, Connelly, she admonished herself. She went into Mickie's room and kissed the little girl good-night, then hurried into her room before Justin could catch her, if he even intended to.

She didn't bother with a shower, and instead changed right into her nightie. No way was she going to risk going out there and running into Justin again.

She flipped out the light and in a few minutes heard

his tread up the stairs. It sounded as if he hesitated outside her door but then went on. She wasn't sure. She was thankful he hadn't knocked if he had indeed passed by.

Oh, how she was thankful. She'd had no business kissing Justin like that. She was his employee, nothing more. No wonder he looked shocked.

True, he had initiated the kiss. Was it possible he'd felt responsible for what had happened at the restaurant and had thought to apologize, then reacted to the yearning for him he'd seen in her eyes? Or maybe it had just been one of those fluke things. After all, there was a full moon tonight, and full moons made people go crazy, didn't they?

She pulled the covers over her head. She didn't want to think about it. She couldn't think about it. She had just come out of a bad relationship with André, a man she'd *thought* she'd loved, though she realized now she had just enjoyed his company.

André was sweet, but there had never been a real spark between them. He certainly hadn't caused the reaction in her that Justin had just caused.

No, she would not compare them. Justin was... Justin. Her brother-in-law and her employer. That was all. And he would stay that. She would make sure to forget what had happened, then he wouldn't have to look so shocked again.

Yes, that's what she'd do. She couldn't afford to get close to someone else a second time. She knew he'd forgiven her for the past, but he wouldn't forgive her if he found out she was infertile. He would believe that was the only reason she'd come back in the first place. And he'd be basically right. She wouldn't be able to argue, and he'd throw her out and probably refuse to allow her to see Mickie again. There would be hurt all around.

Dear Father, what have I done? Please, please, please help me to ignore my feelings and just do the job I came here to do.

She admitted she'd wanted to get to know Mickie and Justin, too—but not that way. Only hurt could come of it. She touched her lips, recalling their kiss, then gasped when she realized what she was doing.

Burrowing her head under her pillow, she vowed that tomorrow she would force herself to forget what had happened tonight. Yes, as the old saying went, tomorrow was another day. She'd start fresh, avoid Justin if necessary. But she would, in no way, let him think she was interested in more than a working relationship...no matter what her heart and lips were telling her.

Chapter Thirteen

"**I**'m a singing angel!"

Sarah swung around from the counter, where she was putting the finishing touch on a bowl of potato salad. Mickie bounced into the kitchen from the garage door, Justin right behind her.

Looking as handsome as ever. Almost two weeks after that kiss and she couldn't seem to stop noticing how good he looked. He wore a pair of well-worn jeans, boots and a soft tan shirt with a darker pullover sweater. His hair was tousled from the crisp, cool November wind and his cheeks had just a hint of color.

"My little angel. Of course she sings," Justin teased.

"No, Daddy," Mickie said, exasperation in her voice. "Daddy took me by the school today to see the posted list—after we got the cranberries for the meal—and my name was under the singing angels! Aunt Sarah, can you make my costume?"

Sarah, who was smiling happily at her niece, suddenly winced. "Um, honey..." She trailed off.

Justin, evidently seeing her dilemma, scooped up his daughter and gave her whisker brushes against her cheeks, earning a squeal. "If Auntie Sarah can't, we'll find someone who can, pumpkin."

Sarah felt she'd let Mickie down—and Justin, if he felt he had to distract his daughter—so, she piped up, "I can certainly go to school and see what the other parents are doing and if I don't think I can, then I'll find you someone, sweetie. Is that a deal?"

Mickie squirmed from her daddy's grasp, then ran over and wrapped her arms around Sarah's legs, almost overturning her. "Deal," she said.

The doorbell rang.

"I'll get it," Mickie yelled, heading for the door at a dead run.

For the first time in over a week, Sarah was alone with Justin. His scrutiny made her nervous. To cover her unease, she turned back to the counter and stirred the potato salad. Justin had picked up the rest of the food from a local restaurant. All she had to make was potato salad, then serve what Bill and his wife brought.

Justin started forward and she stiffened. There had been an uncomfortable truce since the night she'd run off and hidden in her room. She wasn't looking forward to discussing it. She'd thought maybe Justin had regretted it as much as she did. After all, he had suddenly had all these extra hours he'd had to put in. It was only last night when she'd called Justin for something that Christine had mentioned he always doubled his hours just before Thanksgiving and Christmas. She said it was to catch up so he could have free time.

Now, with the look on his face and the way he was approaching, she was afraid he was going to broach the subject of their embrace. A subject she'd prefer to leave undiscussed.

The sound of the door whooshing open was a relief. No longer alone, she felt safe to relax. Arms snaked around her and she jumped, before she realized it wasn't Justin. "Hi there, sweetheart, gotta hug for me?"

"Bill!" Sarah turned in his arms and gave him an enthusiastic hug.

He chuckled. "Gonna have my wife scalping me if you don't watch it."

"And where is she?" Sarah demanded, stepping back. "I haven't seen her in at least three months."

"I've been keeping her busy taking care of me since we got married." He nodded and shook Justin's hand. "She's playing with Mickie. Here are some deviled eggs," he said, handing Sarah a platter covered with foil. "I'll be right back with the ham."

He paused at the door and winked. "I just might have an announcement later that you'll be interested in. Come on, Justin, say hi to Marcy while I get the ham."

Justin followed him out. Sarah was relieved. She put the platter on the counter next to the potato salad and went to the sink to wash her hands. The door whooshed back open. "Just place the ham on the counter, Bill, and I'll let Justin cut it up."

"Unfortunately, I'm not Bill."

Sarah whirled, slinging water over the countertop. She grabbed a towel to wipe her hands and mop up the mess, remembering to turn off the water as she did. Only a moment of silence lingered before Justin sauntered over and leaned against the counter near her.

"Why do I have a feeling you'd be more comfortable if I *were* Bill?"

"That's not true," she said, but didn't lift her eyes.

"You've been avoiding me," he said softly.

"No!" she denied quickly.

"Yes," he countered quietly.

She shrugged, not liking the look in his eyes. Oh, why had she avoided him and let the unknown build between them? She didn't like confrontations anymore. Not with him. Justin always won.

"Does this have to do with the other night?"

"No," she denied again, lifting her chin and meeting his eyes.

A gleam appeared in his eyes at her challenging stance. "Yes," he whispered.

"If you have all the answers, why ask?" she demanded, disagreeably.

"I have a feeling this has to do with that guilt thing again," he said, stepping closer.

He was right. How did he know she was feeling guilty for practically attacking him on his own doorstep? She refused to answer, mutely staring at him.

"Tic tac toe?" he said, turning to where his hip was leaning against the counter. He dropped his arms, allowing his right elbow to rest on the counter. "Three no's in a row?"

With his left hand, he reached out and snagged her

elbow to keep her from backing any farther away. "You've nothing to feel guilty about unless you were only kissing me out of obligation."

Sarah saw the sudden watchful gaze in his eyes and realized he really didn't know how she felt. Though she wouldn't enlighten him on the latter, she would put his mind at ease on the former. "No," she whispered, aching at the thought of ever intentionally hurting this man's feelings again.

"Good," he said, and satisfaction shone in his eyes. Before she knew what he was doing, he grabbed both her arms and pulled her forward. "Because I've wanted to do this again since that night."

He lowered his head and pressed his lips to hers.

He felt so good. His arms slid around her and his head turned, slanting gently across her mouth as he expertly showed her exactly how much he enjoyed sharing this kiss.

Sarah trembled even as she held on to handfuls of his sweater and returned the kiss. This felt so good, so right. He was gentle, tender, demanding, patient. He was perfect.

"Ahem."

Sarah pushed back and dazedly glanced toward the source of the noise. She immediately flushed when she saw Bill standing there, nonchalantly leaning against the counter near the door. "Excuse me," she said. She grabbed the potato salad and headed into the other room.

The door swished shut behind her. The silence was thick for a moment before Bill finally asked, "Did I see what I thought I saw?"

"You saw a kiss," Justin replied.

"Oh, yeah, Justin. I saw a kiss...and much more. The look on your face is more than just a kiss."

Justin stiffened, but Bill held up a hand. "Hey, I think it's great. But she *is* living here."

Justin sighed and ran a weary hand through his hair. "I agree this isn't the best situation. I know it's important to avoid all appearance of impropriety. However, I've given this over two weeks of thought, Bill.

"Mrs. Winters will be home in another week or two. I talked with her last night. She's more than willing to come back here on a part-time basis until I can find a new sitter. I have a couple of openings coming up at work, jobs that Sarah is qualified for that will give her enough money to afford a place of her own."

"Wow," Bill said, low. "That serious, huh?"

Justin nodded. "I think so."

"So, what about until then?" he asked.

Justin turned toward the window and stared out. "We're both adults. We're both Christian, with moral values. We know how to behave, even though we're attracted to each other."

"Said Adam to God just before Eve showed up."

"Very funny," Justin said when Bill chuckled.

"I'm sorry," Bill replied. "Look, I love you both. You're like a brother and Sarah is like a sister. I'd hate for anything to happen between you that you'd regret later."

"We have a sitter. Mickie, if you've forgotten."

"Who has an earlier bedtime," Bill reminded him. "Anyway, if things get too intense, please twist Sarah's arm to take that garage apartment that's empty at my house. I've told her she's always welcome. Hey, I'll admit she wouldn't take it before, but I just bet she'd let me help her out now.''

Justin turned back to his friend. ''Thanks, Bill. I will.''

The door swung open and Sarah warily walked back into the kitchen. ''So, do I get to watch the football game here?'' Bill asked Justin.

Justin groaned. ''As long as it's Dallas we watch.''

''You know that's not my team.''

Sarah hurried past, grabbed some other dishes, shot a glance at both men, then gave Bill a dark look. ''You wanna eat, help me set the table.'' She went back out.

Bill grinned, grabbed some of the dishes and said, ''She knows I was reading you the riot act.''

Justin picked up the platter of eggs. ''She knows and she doesn't like anyone interfering in her life.''

''So sue me,'' he said, and followed Sarah out the door.

Sarah decided the meal went fine. Thanksgiving was a joyous occasion, she thought, smiling wistfully, especially when it was shared with family and friends. André's family had been so formal, exchanging only polite talk. Here, there was joking and any subject was open for debate.

And joke telling was the most popular, especially when she and Mickie got into a contest to see who could come up with the corniest jokes.

''Hey, Aunt Sarah, April showers bring May flowers. What do *Mayflowers* bring?''

Sarah looked stumped.

Everyone else at the table said in unison, "Pilgrims!"

Sarah chuckled. "Please no more, dear. You beat me hands down on the jokes."

Mickie giggled.

Bill interrupted the gaiety with a big smile. "Well, I can't think of a better time to tell our news than now, when we're with our spiritual family, can you, Marcy?"

Sarah was smiling, but at the sudden glow in Marcy's eyes, Sarah's smile froze. Bill and Marcy had been married only three months. Surely their news couldn't be...

"Well, come on," Justin said. "Don't keep us in suspense."

Bill grabbed Marcy's hand. "Marcy is due the last part of June. We're gonna have a baby."

"Congratulations!" Justin exclaimed, jumping up and slapping Bill on the back.

"Congratulations," Sarah echoed, smiling at Marcy, even though the edge of her vision was turning black.

She hadn't realized someone else's news would hurt so much. Of course, it was the first time she'd been confronted with this since her own news.

"Why do you have to wait till June?" Mickie demanded.

Marcy smiled. "Well, it takes that long for the baby in my tummy to get big enough to be born."

Mickie immediately jumped up and ran around the table. Looking at her stomach, she studied it a long moment. Finally, she asked, "How'd it get in there?"

Bill laughed.

Marcy turned pink.

"We'll discuss that later, sweetheart," Justin said.

"Maybe when I get a brother or sister of my own?" she asked.

It was Justin's turn to blush.

Sarah felt like throwing up. With as good a smile as she could manage, she stood. "I'll be right back."

She headed toward the back of the house for the guest bathroom. But that wasn't where she was going. She wanted to be alone. After slipping into the darkened study, she softly closed the door behind her.

As soon as she was sure she wouldn't be overheard, she broke down. *Why, God? Why? I don't begrudge Marcy her child. I'm happy for her and Bill. But I'm jealous too, envious, even hurt. Why won't I ever have children of my own?*

Deep racking sobs shook her body and she cried out all her pain and rage. *It doesn't seem fair. I love children. I've always wanted children. Why?*

She ranted and raved within as she reached out to heaven in beseeching appeal. Finally, a peace settled into her heart and she knew that no matter what, she would serve God. Sometimes, she wouldn't know the reasons here on Earth, but one day, in heaven, she'd know, and understand why the doctor had this diagnosis.

She found the box of tissues, blew her nose and tried to repair her makeup. She knew she'd been gone too long but hoped she'd have time to sneak upstairs and cover her blotchy red face before anyone found her.

However, even that small peace was denied her as the door opened behind her. She could only hope it was Mickie.

"Sarah?"

It just *had* to be Justin.

"Um-hmm?" she answered, afraid her voice would give away her crying jag.

The door shut behind him. "What's the matter? I could tell something troubled you at the table."

She kept her head down as Justin approached. When he placed his hand under her chin and urged her to look up, she resisted. But she could tell he wasn't going to take no for an answer.

Slowly, she allowed him to lift her face to his scrutiny. "Oh, Sarah," he said, concern etching his voice. "What happened to cause this?"

She shrugged, his compassion nearly releasing a fresh flood of tears.

"When Marcy announced—"

He got no further. She stiffened.

"What?" he asked determinedly, though he said it with a gentle insistence.

"Nothing."

"Is it Marcy or maybe Bill?" His eyes widened. "Surely you're not jealous that Bill is married and having a baby."

"No!" she denied, but could tell he was still suspicious that he'd found the answer. "Honestly," she said, because now it was true. She had been jealous and envious for a moment. But now she was just sad, aching for something she would never have.

He wasn't going to believe her unless she told him

the truth. She could already see him mentally pulling away. She should let him. It would be best for both of them. No, it would be best for her. It would hurt him unnecessarily. "I just want kids and don't have any," she finally admitted, feeling fresh tears in her eyes.

"Oh, Sarah," he murmured, and pulled her into his arms.

This time she couldn't control the tears that wet the front of his shirt as he stroked her back and her hair over and over, murmuring and praying as she cried her heart out anew.

Slowly, her tears subsided. Justin continued to hold her. Lifting her tear-drenched face, she whispered rawly, "I'm so sorry you saw me this way."

Tenderly, he shook his head. "Never, ever apologize for your pain, Sarah. We all have pain and it hurts us to hold it in, especially as painful as yours seems to be. God put us on this Earth and told us to bear one another's burdens. I'm here for you. Bill is, too. And Marcy. As is my pastor, who happens to adore you, you know. Never, ever think you have to hold such a load by yourself."

He stroked her cheek and she was so thankful for the man she'd come to work for. He was more than just a brother-in-law, much more than she'd thought he was back when she'd first met him. He was the man she loved.

Her heart flip-flopped at the realization.

She loved him.

And she was infertile.

That could have easily brought on a new round of

crying if he hadn't chosen that moment to lower his head and kiss her. He feathered his mouth over hers, then over her eyes, her cheeks and finally her mouth again.

What he gave her in his kiss felt like life-giving nectar for a starving soul.

"Bill told me I could come check on you."

Mickie's small voice at the door caused them both to break apart. Once again Sarah was mortified, until she heard Justin's dark reply, "Thank you, Bill."

A giggle escaped her. Justin sighed and abruptly sat down on the couch. His reaction pulled another, then another, giggle out of her.

Soon Justin's strained chuckle joined her voice and the tension was relieved.

But Sarah knew, deep down, the problems had just begun.

Chapter Fourteen

At the sound of the doorbell, Sarah came jogging down the stairs. "That's probably the lady with the pattern for your outfit, Mickie," Sarah said as Mickie dashed from the kitchen. "The president of the PTA promised to have someone bring it to me today, even if it is the day after Thanksgiving."

"I'll get it!" Mickie cried, grabbing the door even as Justin came out of the kitchen, where he and Mickie had been making cookies.

Sarah slowed her sprint to a sedate walk, not wanting to be caught running down the stairs.

Justin grinned and smiled giving her a "I know that bad habit from Mickie and you can't trick me" look.

She reached the front door just as Mickie swung it open. And Sarah wished she'd stayed upstairs and let Justin handle it.

"Come on in, Miss Stephanie."

Stephanie smiled her saccharine-sweet smile and maneuvered her way inside. "Why, hello, Sarah. I bet you didn't expect it to be me who brought this by, but I told Mary Ann that I just lived right around the corner practically and knew you wouldn't want to get out—well, hi, Justin,'' she said, feigning shock. ''What are you doing home today?''

Sarah sighed and took the pattern Stephanie thrust in her hands as she walked past.

''It is the day after Thanksgiving, Mrs.—Stephanie,'' he said.

As if the woman hadn't known he'd be here, Sarah thought, disgusted.

''Well, Mary Ann told me Sarah had called with concerns about the outfit for Mickie and I just had to come over to make sure Mickie was going to get what she needed. It's such a shame she doesn't have someone who can sew and do all those little things for her. Isn't that right, sweetheart?'' Stephanie cooed to Mickie, who had come over to get the pattern and look at it.

Sarah wanted to hug Mickie when she said, ''Oh, Aunt Sarah will take care of everything,'' and then beamed up at her.

Stephanie only looked disconcerted for a moment before turning back to Justin. ''I hope you had a nice Thanksgiving. Though my husband is dead, I make sure to cook a fresh turkey every year with all the trimmings. I feel it's important for the children to experience traditions, not the store-bought things so many people are serving up these days.''

Did the woman have a spy watching their every move? Sarah wondered with displeasure. Stephanie could make her feel a failure faster than any other woman she knew. And Justin just stood there and smiled politely. It was really nauseating.

"We had friends over," Justin said.

"You had friends over? I'm sure they appreciated your housekeeper's cooking, then."

Justin, thankfully, didn't rise to the bait. He smiled. "We had an enjoyable time."

"I must say, the house has stood up tolerably well, considering poor little Mickie has only had a string of sitters. You've done an admirable job. You should also be very proud of the part she got in the play. Not all the little girls are getting to be a front-row angel."

Sarah rolled her eyes. This cooing over Justin was going to go on forever. And she refused to stand here and listen to it while being purposely ignored by the woman. With a smile, she said, "Excuse me. I have some chores to take care of."

Justin narrowed his eyes slightly, but Stephanie looked smug. Sarah merely smiled sweetly, patted Mickie as she walked past where she clung to her daddy's leg and headed up the stairs.

Sarah did have work to do. Maybe it was wrong to leave the way she had, but she didn't like standing there watching another woman coo over Justin.

Mickie said it was tradition to get down the Christmas ornaments the day after Thanksgiving and she'd looked so wistful that Sarah hadn't been able to resist. Since Justin had offered to make cutout cookies with Mickie—something Sarah had never done before— Sarah had decided to explore the attic and surprise Mickie with the ornaments. She had just pulled down the ladder to the attic that was located at the end of the hallway near Justin's room, when the doorbell had rung.

She'd rather be searching for ornaments than listening to Stephanie.

She climbed up the attic and moved boxes around until she found one labeled "Christmas." With a sigh she pulled it out. Just as she was about to open it, she found a smaller one, farther back, covered in dust and spider webs. She supposed as housekeeper, cleaning the attic would fall to her, too. It certainly needed it. This one said "X-mas" on it. But this one, unlike the other one, was labeled in Amy's handwriting.

Sarah pulled it out and opened it.

Well, she'd found the ornaments. Fond memories assailed her as she pulled them out. Each girl had her own collection of ornaments as they'd grown up. Their mother had said it was a tradition they should keep and that when they married, their first tree would have memories on it.

Amy had been much more creative than Sarah. She had made her own ornaments each year, in addition to the one her parents would buy her. One by one Sarah pulled them out and touched them, remembering how they had been lovingly crafted.

"Those were Amy's."

Sarah looked up to see Justin's head and shoulders poking through the entrance. "Mickie's playing Nintendo. I was looking for you and saw the ladder down."

"Running from Stephanie?" A soft smile curved her lips.

"Thank you for leaving me there with her," he

muttered darkly, and came up the stairs. "She's gone, too. I told her I had to find my housekeeper and explain the rules of decorum."

"You didn't!" Sarah gasped.

He chuckled. "Consider yourself properly chastised."

She chuckled. "I promised Mickie I'd get these down for her. She said you always brought them out of the attic the day after Thanksgiving."

"Not those," he said.

Sarah's hands stilled. "I don't understand."

Justin pulled over a small trunk and sat down next to her. He took the small tan cloth ornament with a Christmas tree cross-stitched on it. "I haven't used these since Amy died."

"I'm so sorry." Sarah realized her blunder. "I saw this box." She indicated the nearer one. "And then this one. I just thought you must have kept your ornaments separate."

He rubbed his thumb over the material. "She was so proud of these. They were so filled with memories for her. The year she died, well, it was only a week after Thanksgiving and I just couldn't bring myself to use her ornaments. We went out and bought all new ones."

"Oh, Justin," she whispered, her heart breaking. She started to reach for the ornament he had, but he stopped her.

Taking the box from her lap, he began to go through it. "This one she said she made when she was sixteen." He held up two hearts entwined.

Sarah chuckled. "She was certain she was in love

and was going to stitch the names in there when the boy declared himself.''

Rummaging through the box, he found another one. "She made this one when Mickie was born.''

A cradle with the year on it in blues and greens graced the front of the small stuffed pillow-shaped ornament. "It's beautiful.''

She fingered one and tears touched her eyes. "This was one of my favorites.'' She held up one with a cross that had a cradle in front of it. "She made this one the year she asked Jesus into her heart.''

Justin sighed, put the other ornaments back into the box, then dropped his head. "You know, Sarah, I really loved Amy. It was a comfortable, caring relationship, one I went into because I thought she loved me.''

"I know,'' Sarah replied. And though it sounded funny for her to be saying that to Justin, she realized it was the truth. No matter what she'd thought in the past, she knew Justin wasn't the type to marry Amy out of a sense of obligation or guilt. She silently asked why her parents had encouraged Amy to marry him. It had only ended up hurting everyone involved. Amy just didn't know how to say no. The only time she had tried, she'd died out on a lonely road, alone. "I miss her.''

Justin slipped an arm around her and gave Sarah a small squeeze. "I do, too. It was really hard when she first died. There was so much guilt over her death and I had a small child and I didn't know what I was going to do. I blamed Amy for leaving me. But slowly, day after day, I began to function again, and now, when I think about Amy, it's like another lifetime, bittersweet.

I loved her, but we were both young, inexperienced. I was so different. I know she's happy where she is now and the only thing I still grieve over is that Mickie won't know her.''

''She remembers bits and snatches.''

''I wonder if she does or if it's that I remind her.''

He slipped his arm from around her and put the lid on the ornaments. ''Whichever,'' he said, tucking the box under his arm, ''I think it's time to bring these back out and start some new memories of our own.''

''Our own?'' she asked, shocked at what he'd said.

''Mickie and me,'' he said, and looked at her strangely.

Oh, of course. Now, why had she thought he was referring to her? ''I agree. It'll be nice for Mickie to have the ornaments for herself. Our mom said we could do whatever we wanted with our ornaments. And I'm sure Amy would want her daughter to have hers.''

''You have some, too?''

Sarah flushed. ''Yes. Both Amy and I did.''

''Would you like to add them to the tree?''

Sarah immediately shook her head. ''No. They'd get mixed up when it was time to take the tree down, and well, they're in storage and everything.''

She would've sworn Justin looked disappointed. ''Well, if you'd like to see them,'' she offered shyly.

''That'd be great!'' He stood. ''Let me push the other box over to the entrance, then I'll stand below to catch it.''

''You sure you don't have Stephanie down there to watch your macho show of strength,'' she teased.

"Maybe you've considered remarriage and think you have to impress her."

He paused by the stairs and turned back to her. There was no teasing glint in his eyes. No, he looked very serious when he said, "Stephanie is mainly attracted to my bank account. I can guarantee you, I'll only be marrying someone who can love me in the truest sense of the word."

The look in his eyes sent a shiver of awareness through her. She nervously licked her lips and wiped her hands on her jeans. Oh, she could love him in the truest sense of the word, and easily, but she wondered if he could love her when he found out her secret.

The sound of Mickie thudding up the stairs, and her voice, broke the spell, "Telephone, Aunt Sarah!"

She smiled, albeit shakily. "Saved by the bell."

He smiled back. "Only a reprieve, Sarah. We'll have to discuss these emotions bouncing around between us sooner or later."

She climbed down the stairs, then ran to the library so she could have some privacy. She couldn't think of who had the phone number here, or even who would be calling her.

"I want to know what you told your boss that caused him to take his business away from my firm." The nasty voice of Drydan Watson reverberated through the phone.

"I don't know what you're talking about."

"Oh, don't play dumb with me, missy. I know you're wrapping Justin around your little finger. That's the only reason he'd trade a reputable firm such as mine for a smaller, no-name outfit. I purposely didn't call his work today but instead called you to warn you that if you don't do something to get Watson and Watson back in his good graces, your little secret is going to be out.''

Sarah, who had been stunned by hearing his voice, now got angry. ''Go ahead and tell him, Drydan. It doesn't matter to me.''

''When you lose your power over him it will. After all, who's paying your bills, letting you live in his house, eat his food and who knows what else under his roof? It'll matter plenty if you don't do something. I'll give you until the first of January. After all, with the holidays, he won't have much time to get anything done. But come January 1, if you haven't convinced Justin that everything you've said about my family is lies, he's going to know your guilty little secret.''

The phone slammed in her ear.

Slowly, she replaced her receiver. So Justin had let Drydan Watson go. Was it because of what she'd told him? Justin had certainly been furious.

For some reason, that brought a bit of joy to her heart. Justin had actually defended her by dropping Drydan and hiring someone else. A silly grin spread across her face. If she hadn't loved him before, she certainly did now.

Why would he do such a thing over Drydan's stupid tantrums? She knew Drydan Watson would get over his anger and things would go on. He only stepped on those smaller than him or those who threatened him in some way. She'd been a threat to his son, so he'd made sure to stomp out that threat. But now she was a threat to him through Justin's business.

Her smile left her face. That meant Drydan just might reveal her secret to Justin in order to get even.

"Hey, I forgot to ask you what I'd wanted to when I hunted you down earlier."

Sarah whirled, finding Justin at the door.

"Are you okay? Bad news?" He indicated the telephone by cutting his eyes to the instrument, then back to her.

"No. No, you just startled me."

His smile returned. "Well, I remember what it was that I forgot when I saw the ornaments."

He came into the room, brushing at his light blue sweater, then wiping his hands on his jeans. "The decorations are only part of the tradition. I'm a firm believer in traditions and I've decided Mickie is old enough to appreciate a live Christmas tree."

He pulled his wallet out of the desk and stuffed it in his back pocket. "So this year I've decided it's time to take Mickie to a Christmas-tree farm. I thought she would really enjoy it. What do you think?"

Sarah nodded. "She'd love it. We always begged our parents for a real tree, but they hated the pine needles."

Justin smiled. "I have a housekeeper. I don't have to worry about cleaning up pine needles."

"Thanks a lot," she said, laughing.

"Good. Grab your jacket or sweater. It's cool out today. I'll get Mickie's pullover and we can go. We should get there just about sunset."

"You want me to go with you?" Sarah asked, surprised.

Justin had the audacity to look affronted. "Of

course I do. Who else will I be able to pawn Mickie off on if she gets too excited over this new event?''

''Again, thank you,'' Sarah said, though she wasn't upset. She was actually very excited to be included.

Justin smiled his smug smile. ''Anytime. Now go! I'll get the four-by-four warmed up.''

Chapter Fifteen

"A real-live Christmas tree?" Mickie exclaimed as Justin drove the truck into the tree lot.

"That's right. Any one you decide on," Justin said.

Sarah shot him a warning look. "But I bet you'd sure like your daddy's opinion."

Mickie nodded. "I know exactly what I want. It's got to be big, and just right."

The vehicle stopped and she jumped out. Sarah was slower pushing open her front door, but she was just as excited. Justin chuckled and slid out his side of the truck. "You both look awed."

"I've never been here. I didn't know they grew trees in rows," she said, regarding the lines and lines of trees. "I thought this was just a piece of property and you had to go out and hunt in the forest."

"You've been neglected." He tsked, took a hand-saw from the person at the gate, then caught up to where his daughter impatiently waited for them. "They have a hay ride and a gift shop and a place where you can order special trees, and even some trees, that have been shipped from up north—trees you normally wouldn't see down here. Come on.''

The person told them where everything was located and they started down the paths. ''Oh, here's one, Daddy,'' Mickie immediately exclaimed, stopping in front of a tree not quite four feet high. ''Except that it's not as tall as you and it's got a big hole in the daddy branches.''

''Daddy branches?'' Justin asked.

''Yeah, you know, daddy branches.'' She pointed at another one. ''The mama branches have a hole in that one.''

''Honey, I don't know what you mean, either,'' Sarah said as she hurried behind the young girl, trying to keep step with Justin.

''You know, daddy, mama and children branches. That's how my teacher explained it.''

When Sarah shrugged Mickie explained. ''Daddy branches hold up the mama branches and mama branches hold up the children branches, then the baby branch goes on top for the star.''

Sarah was still confused, but Justin had evidently caught on. Mickie grabbed his hand and stood him next to a tree to compare the height, then shook her head and walked on.

''You wanna translate, Justin?'' Sarah asked, trailing along beside them.

''She's got quite an interesting teacher. They have an artificial tree at school and I imagine she means the A-shape of the tree, the larger branches on the bottom being the daddy branches and so on.''

Light dawned in Sarah's eyes, then she lifted an eyebrow in disbelief. "That's what they're teaching kids in school?"

Justin shrugged. "I guess it's a way to explain the family unit or something. As I said, this teacher is very inventive. Had Mickie not been in her class all year, I would've been stumped, too. But this explanation of a tree is mild compared with some of the things Mickie has told me."

Mickie stopped him several more times but found fault with each tree. It was finally Sarah who noted it was almost completely dark out, that gently suggested a tree to Mickie. "Oh, yes, Aunt Sarah. This one is perfect. My own mama couldn't have picked out a more perfect tree. See how much taller it is than Daddy. It reaches way up and will almost touch the sky."

"And our ceiling," Justin murmured.

"You can cut it if it's too big," Sarah said, afraid they'd end up on another trek if Mickie changed her mind.

"Right there, Daddy. Cut it."

Justin crawled underneath the tree and began to saw. "Wait a minute, it's tipping," Sarah warned, reaching out for it. "Get back, Mickie, so it won't fall on you."

Sarah leaned over the large branches and grabbed near the top to try to steady the tree. She realized too late how far off balance this put her. "Watch out, Justin!"

She jerked back, but too late. The weight of the falling tree propelled her forward. She let out a squeak and landed right on top of the tree, which had fallen directly on top of Justin.

A grunt was all she heard. She tried to scramble off the tree as gingerly as possible.

"Watch it, will you?"

"Oh," he groaned as she scooted backward.

She shoved at the tree until it was out of the way. Justin lay on the soft needle-covered ground, thankfully in one piece. "I'm sorry?" She said it more as a question than a statement.

"I suppose you are, since I'm holding the car keys and you'd be stuck here if you did me under. Here, help me up," he said, extending his hand.

Mickie laughed. "You look funny, Daddy. You've got pine needles in your hair."

"Thanks, kid," he said, smiling.

He swiped at his hair but missed most of the needles, so Sarah moved forward and brushed at them. His hands stilled and his eyes met hers.

"Come on, Daddy. Let's take the tree home!"

Justin's gaze left Sarah's. "How about we let them tie this to the top of the car, then we go on a hay ride."

"Oh, cool!" Mickie clapped her hands, jumping up and down. "The church hay ride's in October, but I didn't get to go because I was too little. I'm not too little, am I, Daddy?"

He shook his head. "I saw a baby on one when we drove in and you're certainly not a baby anymore."

Mickie was almost dancing in excitement. Sarah smiled and followed Justin and the little girl to the front part of the building. "Can we look in the store while you get the tree taken care of?'' she asked Justin.

''Sure. Meet me out here.'' He looked indulgently at his daughter before heading off toward the car.

Sarah and Mickie went into the small shop and walked up and down the aisles.

''Oh, look, Aunt Sarah.'' Mickie touched a necklace with a red heart and green bells. ''Isn't it just so pretty?''

''I'll tell you what. You need something to remind you of your trip here. What if I buy you that and you can wear it outside and show your daddy.''

''I like that.'' Mickie picked it up and turned it back and forth to admire every angle.

''I think I'll buy myself a bell necklace, too. Want to take these over to the counter, then go watch for your daddy so he won't miss seeing us?''

Mickie immediately obeyed. When she was gone, Sarah bought two other things that had caught her attention. One was a small round glass ornament painted with two hearts and green confetti in the background—Mickie would love that as a surprise under the tree—and the other was a cup with a picture of a man toting a Christmas tree on his back. It was dated with the current year.

She went to the counter, paid for the things and dropped the surprises in her purse. ''Here, Mickie,'' she called, and draped the necklace around the little girl's neck. Dropping the long satin string of the other necklace over her own neck, she giggled at Mickie's incredulous expression.

''It almost touches your jeans,'' Mickie noted.

"That it does. But I like odd-looking jewelry. Let's go find your daddy."

He was at the car, assisting the men in tying the tree down. Sarah dropped her purse in the car, then locked the door.

"My," Justin drawled, staring down at his daughter, "what have we here?"

"Isn't it just the most beautiful necklace you've ever seen, Daddy?"

She held it up, turning it back and forth so Justin could get a good look. "You know what I think? The most beautiful girl I've ever seen is wearing it, so that makes it beautiful."

Mickie giggled and rolled her eyes before skipping toward where a few couples were just climbing onto the flatbed truck filled with hay.

"I like your necklace, too," Justin said and reached out and lifted it away from Sarah's neck. It was getting dark. He wasn't close enough for her to see his expression.

"We'd better catch Mickie before they leave us," she said to cover her nervousness.

He dropped the necklace. "I doubt she'd miss us."

"But I'd miss the ride."

He chuckled. "You're as bad as she is."

"And you're not having fun?" she asked, hurrying over to the truck.

Justin lifted his daughter in. "I just love having a tree squish me," he said dryly.

She stepped up and felt his hands on her waist, steadying her. Her heart rate accelerated. She didn't comment but went to where Mickie sat right at the back of the cab of the truck.

Justin seated himself next to her and willingly accepted Mickie's squeezing in between them. A helpless smile filled his eyes, which were only inches away from her. His look said *I tried.*

Sarah felt flattered. There was no doubt after today that Justin was acting more than just brotherly toward her. She had a feeling he had actually begun to like her. He might even be interested in her, if she wasn't mistaken.

She was surprised she didn't think of André and miss him when Justin smiled at her. No, instead she thought only of how perfect Justin was for her and how wonderful it was to be out from under the constant strain of André being so passive and compliant whenever his parents had criticized her.

She still hadn't forgotten that Justin had let Drydan Watson go, after what she had told him. She felt a little guilty. After all, what had happened to her had nothing to do with the business end of Justin's life; it had been strictly personal. And she would mention it to Justin—soon, because she didn't want Drydan revealing anything if Justin truly was developing feelings for her. Yes, that was her task to do. Still, it was nice to know he had believed her and taken her side, even though she hadn't asked him to.

The stars twinkled brightly in the sky and the moon was almost full again. It was hard to believe she'd been at Justin's over a month now.

Speakers softly played Christmas music. Couples settled down in the hay, snuggling against the cool crisp wind. Funny that Mickie was the only child on the ride. Maybe because it was after dark and most families had already left the farm.

Mickie wiggled between them. "This hay is poking me."

Justin reached to lift her onto his lap just as the ride started up. Mickie surprised them both by evading her daddy and crawling into Sarah's lap.

"I want Aunt Sarah to hold me."

Sarah's heart expanded as the little girl nestled in her arms, resting her head against Sarah's shoulder. She stretched her legs across Sarah's lap, then frowned at her daddy.

"She's softer."

Justin chuckled. "I imagine she is." But there was a tenderness reflected in his eyes from the small electrical lanterns overhead.

Mickie found a strand of hair that was hanging over Sarah's shoulder and stroked it with her tiny fingers.

"She's tired," Justin murmured, though he sounded just a little choked up over his daughter's need to be held by Sarah.

"Am not!" Mickie piped up, then nestled closer.

Sarah smiled and nodded slightly. She saw the gleaming moisture in Justin's eyes and realized how much it affected him that Mickie didn't have a mother. Sometimes a girl just needed a mom. She wondered how those many motherless children survived without the nurturing care of a mother. She thanked God she'd never had to find out, though she still missed her mom some now, then said a quick prayer that Mickie wouldn't suffer from missing Amy.

As the music of one of her favorite Christmas songs started, she began to hum along with it. The ride rocked them and in less than five minutes Mickie was slumped against her.

"She's asleep," she said softly to Justin, who had been strangely quiet.

"You have a beautiful voice," he murmured.

Sarah blushed and was glad it was dark. "Thank you."

"Please, go ahead, sing some more."

"Oh, I couldn't," she protested.

"For me? You don't have to sing loud enough for anyone else, Sarah. But please, do it for me."

How could she resist?

The song "Away in the Manger" came on and she began to sing. "'Away in the manger no crib for a bed, the little Lord Jesus lay down his swe—'"

They hit a bump and she broke off, tightening her hold on Mickie. Justin moved his daughter's feet and inched closer, then his arm encircled around her. He pulled her snugly against his side. His other hand came around and rested on Mickie's leg.

She continued singing softly, just so he could hear. On the second verse, Justin joined his voice with hers. He loved the feel of her against him, the protectiveness she brought out, the feelings of attraction. But most of all, he just enjoyed her presence. He couldn't imagine his life without her.

When the song was over, Justin turned toward Sarah. He wanted to ask her about coming to work for him, had thought to do it tonight. He knew he was enjoying her too much in his arms and that could lead to dangerous temptations at his house. After all, God had made man and woman to feel attracted to each other. But there were rules. And it was extremely difficult to follow those rules when the woman looked so longingly at him.

So instead of discussing her future, he leaned forward and kissed her, tenderly, gently, a simple sharing. She'd been so tense the past week or so, but tonight Sarah was relaxed, not hiding anything from him. He liked that and wondered if she could read what was in his eyes.

Seeing Mickie sleeping so contentedly in her arms, he remembered her outburst when Bill had shared the news about Marcy. He wondered how she *really* felt about André.

Yes, that concerned him, because sitting here, looking at her like this, he realized he could give his heart to her—if she could simply love him back.

Oh, he realized he was afraid to love again, but he didn't know how to let go of that fear. Or if he should. Should he simply declare his feelings and not worry that she might feel obligated to accept anything from him because he had provided so much for her?

No. He couldn't do it. He needed to know that she had some sort of feelings for him other than gratitude.

"Look, a meteorite!"

He glanced up and saw a streak across the sky. It was gone almost immediately.

"Do you suppose that's what led the Wise Men to Jesus? That or a comet?"

Justin shook his head. "I doubt it. After all, Jesus

was almost two by the time they located him. Maybe it was a supernova."

"I guess the miracle wasn't in what led them there, but that the Scriptures foretold it."

"Yeah, that and the miracle that Jesus was born into the world."

"And lived and died," Sarah added, snuggling closer in his arms.

He smiled warmly, thinking how wonderful it was to know true joy. "And that He rose again."

"And is always here for us. What love that is," Sarah murmured.

"How true. What love He had to provide such a plan of redemption." *Which reminds me,* Justin thought, *that even if Sarah never loves me I have a Heavenly Father who does. He knows my needs and desires and will fulfill them in the way He knows they should be fulfilled.*

The truck slowed and they were back at the beginning point. Justin smiled at Sarah, lifted Mickie from her arms, then assisted Sarah in standing.

"Thank you for the evening," Sarah whispered as they walked toward the car.

"Thank you, Sarah, for sharing it with us. I think Mickie really enjoyed not only the shopping and the tree but your company, as well."

"I enjoyed her, too." She paused by the car door. "And being with you."

Potent words. He could easily picture the two of them together. He forced the thought away. "It was a very nice evening."

He walked around, strapped Mickie into her seat

belt—Mickie simply sighed and continued to sleep—
then slipped into his own seat.

He turned on a music station that was playing
Christmas music, then backed out of the parking place.

"Why don't you rest. It'll take us at least forty-five
minutes to get back."

"I'll try," she murmured, sounding sleepy.

He shook himself, trying to get rid of the romantic
thoughts going around in his head. They both needed
time to let this relationship develop. And he'd make
sure they had it. Control. He would just have to control
his impulses until he was certain Sarah knew what she
wanted.

Whatever happened between them, he knew one
thing: he wanted God's will. That was the most important thing. He had to let God show him the answers.

Chapter Sixteen

"Are you sure you want me going to the holiday open house?" Sarah asked Justin, pulling on her coat as she came down the stairs.

Justin smiled. "I'd like you there as…protection."

"And just why do you need protection?"

He gave her a look of mock outrage. "People like Stephanie," he said. "There are three different ladies who have marked me single and seek me out any time I'm within two blocks of the school."

Sarah chuckled, and Justin smiled at the sound. He enjoyed listening to Sarah when she was happy. Her eyes sparkled and her whole demeanor radiated energy when she was in a good mood.

"Daddy, I can't go. I've got a tummy ache."

Justin turned at the sound of his daughter's voice. Mickie, dressed in her red-and-green holiday outfit, had a hand on her tummy and stood near the hallway to his library.

"When did this happen?" Justin asked, concerned,

going to her and dropping onto one knee. He felt her head. It was cool. He checked her color, which was normal. Then he looked into her eyes. That was when he knew something else was going on.

''A while ago,'' Mickie mumbled.

Sarah walked up and stroked Mickie's head, going down on one knee by Justin. ''I can stay home with her if you think this is serious.''

Mickie's eyes brightened.

Justin's suspicions deepened. Sometimes when Mickie didn't want to go to school she said she had a tummy ache. But he'd thought they were through that stage.

He wondered if maybe the teacher had sent home a note that he'd never gotten. He hesitated a minute, then made his decision. ''Oh, I think Mickie's well enough to go, aren't you, sweetie? If you get sick then we'll just stop by the doctor's and see what he can do to help.''

Mickie lowered her gaze. ''Yes, sir,'' she said, her mouth drooping.

He stood and saw Sarah's distress. Silently, he shook his head, indicating she shouldn't say anything else.

''Come on, pumpkin, let me carry you to the car. You've been running ahead of me lately and I still like to carry my little girl once in a while.''

Mickie smiled, though she was still subdued. Walking toward the car, he placed a smacking kiss on her cheek. ''Did I tell you today how much I love you?''

''Maybe,'' she replied, her eyes dropping.

''No matter what, you're the most important girl in

my life. Nothing could ever change that.'' He let her down and she climbed into the car.

Sarah gave him a questioning look, but he didn't explain. She decided to change the subject. ''It sure is cold out tonight. Do you think it might snow?''

Mickie brightened considerably. ''Do you think we could make a snowman? Have you ever made a snowman, Aunt Sarah?''

''Oh, my, yes. It's been so many years, though, since we've had real snow around Christmas. You know what I wish? I wish we have a snowy Christmas so we can build a huge snowman.''

''Well, we've got a couple of more weeks until Christmas, so you can keep wishing.''

''So, Mickie, what do you want for Christmas?''

Mickie suddenly quieted.

''What? No wishes?''

''Wishes don't come true if you tell them, do they?''

Justin saw Sarah smile, as if remembering her childhood. ''Well, I know you're not supposed to tell them, but sometimes it doesn't matter. Besides, how are you going to get what you want if you don't ask?''

''I wrote a letter to Santa. He'll know.''

Sarah glanced at Justin. Justin shrugged slightly. He hadn't known Mickie could write well enough to write an entire letter. He'd have to find it and see what he could do about fulfilling the list. He had to wonder if the Fashion Kathy Super House he'd bought might be on it.

''Well, I know what I want,'' Sarah announced.

Justin smiled when Mickie asked, ''What?'' as if

Sarah were getting ready to reveal some deep dark secret.

"Actually, I bought it the other day. I wanted perfumed soaps."

"But, Aunt Sarah, you aren't supposed to buy your own presents."

Sarah chuckled. "When you live on your own, you buy your own gifts."

"But you live with us."

Sarah blinked. "Um, well, actually, I *work* for you, sweetie. It's a little different."

Justin was irritated by her explanation. He was also irritated that she obviously had lived alone so long that she'd forgotten what it was like to receive gifts. Or maybe she was just still so upset about André that she didn't think anyone else would care to get her something special.

"We're here," he said, glad to end the subject before they could ask him what he wanted. He was afraid he would end up saying what he wanted more and more since Sarah had moved in. He wanted a wife. And not just any wife. But he refused to face just who it was he wanted. He wouldn't give up that last bit of fight and succumb to the emotions within him. Because if he did and he found out that Sarah couldn't love him back, he wasn't sure they would ever overcome the breach that would make in their relationship.

Mickie was quiet again. When he stopped the car, she jumped out. "Come on, Aunt Sarah, I want you to see the playground first."

Yep, she was definitely in trouble, Justin thought.

"Go on, Sarah. Meet me in the class in about five minutes."

She smiled. "Okay, Mickie, show me the playground."

He walked into the school and headed down the hall toward Mickie's class. The first incident happened only twenty feet beyond the door.

"Hey, great news. I'm happy to hear it."

The assistant coach slapped him on the back as he passed.

Justin started to ask him what he meant, but the man was already talking with someone else.

Great news?

He continued down the hall. Two more people smiled and called out congratulations. Others whispered when he walked past.

Had news of the merger and the additional two hundred jobs it would create for the local community leaked out already? He hadn't wanted it out until everything was finalized, but maybe Phillip had let the cat out of the bag. What odd looks he was getting, he thought as he continued along the hall.

The crowning incident came when the truth was finally revealed. A couple of parents with their children were just leaving Mickie's class as he entered. There were other families around the different displays, but the teacher, Mrs. Bell, focused on him. Her long gray-and-black hair hung down her back, pinned off her face with two combs. Her skin was wrinkled, but her blue eyes twinkled with the joy that only a teacher who had spent thirty years teaching kindergarten and survived could possess. Her flowing floral skirt and long-sleeved white top perfectly fit the graceful, warm image she projected.

"Well, congratulations, Mr. Warner. I was so happy when Mickie shared her news and…ah, well, this must be Mrs. Warner," she said.

Justin turned in surprise. Sarah was standing behind him, trying to cover her bafflement with a small smile. He glanced from Mrs. Bell to Mickie, who was studying the floor. A huge knot formed in the pit of his stomach. Not of anger, but of pain for what his little girl had done.

He knew, he just *knew* what she had told everyone.

"Did I say something wrong?" Mrs. Bell asked.

But he ignored her, intent on his hurting child. Why hadn't he realized she had been so affected by losing her mom?

Kneeling, he tipped his daughter's chin up until she met his gaze. Her eyes were already awash with tears. "Mickie, honey, have you been telling everyone that you have a new mommy?"

He heard Sarah's gasp, heard the teacher's murmured, "Oh, dear," but didn't take his gaze off his daughter.

"She makes me peanut butter-and-jelly sandwiches and fixes me cookies and comes to meet me after school."

"But there's more than that to being a mommy, honey."

"And she hugs me and reads to me. And she smells good," the little girl said, her chin wobbling. "And now she's gonna hate me, isn't she?"

Suddenly, as if it were too much for her, Mickie

turned and ran off down the hall. Justin stood and started after her.

"Let me," Sarah said. "Give me a couple of minutes."

Then she was gone.

"I'm so sorry, Mr. Warner. I had no idea. Mickie came to school one day and said that she had a new mommy, that her aunt Sarah was now her mommy. I just assumed that was Aunt Sarah and that you had married her."

"That was Aunt Sarah," Justin said, "but I haven't married her. I'll check with you later about Mickie's progress. Right now I need to go find her."

He pulled his coat around him and headed down the hall without a single word to anyone. His heart was breaking over the pain he'd seen in Mickie's eyes. He wondered if Sarah was succeeding at removing that look.

Mickie sat at the bottom of the slide, her face buried against her knees, when Sarah caught up with her. Sarah slowed to a walk. "Mickie, honey, may I sit down?"

Mickie shrugged.

Sarah took that as a yes. She picked up the girl and settled her on her lap, sitting on the swing instead of the slide. Mickie burst into fresh sobs. Slowly, Sarah pushed the swing back and forth, a gentle rocking motion as she let Mickie cry. She saw Justin in the shadows near the building but didn't acknowledge his presence. He was staying put and allowing her to handle this, so he'd just have to wait. She was in no hurry.

Finally, Mickie's cries subsided. "I missed my mommy when she died," Sarah finally said. "It made me very sad not to have someone around."

Mickie sniffled. "Daddy's lonely."

"Ah, is that so?"

Mickie nodded. "So am I."

"So am I sometimes. I miss your mommy, too, and wish she'd come back. She could make me laugh and make me mad. We had such fun."

"Did I have fun with her?"

Sarah felt tears well. "Oh, yes, dear. She use to blow bubbles on your tummy and hug you and love you, just as your daddy does now."

"Other kids have mommies." Her little arms squeezed Sarah tighter.

"That's true. And other people don't have mommies, too."

Mickie finally looked up at Sarah. "You mean I'm not the only one who doesn't have a mommy?"

"No, you're not. And I'll tell you something else. It's okay to want another mommy...but the time has to be right. You have to wait until just the right time when your daddy finally asks someone to marry him and be his wife. Then that woman will be your mommy."

"Daddy has to marry her?" She sounded surprised.

"Yes, he does. And then that woman will be your mommy. But she has to be real special and your daddy has to really love her. And it has to be the right time."

"The right day?" Mickie asked, sounding excited.

"The exactly right day," Sarah said, not sure why Mickie had suddenly brightened at her words. "You know, your daddy doesn't run up and ask. It has to be special and he has to propose—ask her to marry him."

"He has to love her, ask her on the right day, then marry her, for me to have a mommy," Mickie repeated softly, then nodded as if she'd come to some great discovery.

Mickie sat there in Sarah's lap as Sarah continued to push the swing back and forth. Finally, in barely a whisper, Mickie asked, "Are you mad at me?"

Sarah chuckled. "Not at all. I'm very proud that you wanted me to be your mommy. But I really like being your aunt. So what do you say if I just be your aunt and we can do the snuggling and cookie making and all the fun stuff until your daddy finds a wife."

Mickie thought about it a minute. "I guess so."

"And how about you go give your daddy hugs. I think he's feeling a little left out."

Justin stepped out of the shadows so Mickie could see him. He bent down and held out his arms.

Mickie ran to him and hugged him hard around the neck. "I'm sorry, Daddy. I'm so sorry. I love you."

Justin rubbed her up and down the back, his deep voice rumbling, but Sarah was unable to make out any words.

"I promise," Mickie said, and hugged her daddy again.

He crooked his head toward the car and started walking, all the while murmuring in his daughter's ear. Sarah silently followed.

In the car, Mickie almost immediately fell asleep.

The radio played lowly in the background, soothing

both Sarah's and Justin's frazzled nerves. Neither spoke.

In minutes Justin was home and he lifted Mickie out of the car. Sarah gathered her purse and Mickie's doll, which she'd left in the back seat, and followed more slowly.

She went in and changed, then went to Mickie's room, placed her doll by her side and gave her a soft kiss good-night.

Then she went downstairs, intending to get a glass of milk before going to bed. Justin was in the kitchen. At the sound of the swinging door being pushed open, he turned.

Pouring her a glass of milk, he said, "Well, what a mess we're in."

Chapter Seventeen

Sarah laughed, a little nervously. "Well, I'm glad I'm not the one who has to face the school tomorrow."

Justin shook his head. "I'm not sure how to handle it. I never realized Amy's death..." He trailed off.

Sarah stepped forward and placed her hand on his arm. He'd taken off his sweater and she could feel his muscles under the long-sleeved shirt bunch. "It's her age. She's meeting other children and their parents and she has recognized the differences. She doesn't really remember Amy. All she knows is she's different. It's normal, Justin. There's no reason to blame yourself."

Justin sighed, moved over to the small kitchen table and looked out into the yard, which was brightened by a security light. "I'm sorry you got caught in the middle of this, Sarah."

Sarah sat down at the table. "No problem. That's what family is for. Besides, she could have told people Stephanie was her new mommy."

Justin groaned. "That's true." He glanced at her

and must have seen something in her eyes, for he suddenly asked, "You aren't feeling guilty, are you?"

She smiled. "It's true I do battle guilt, isn't it? Actually, I'm wondering if Stephanie was right when she inquired the other day if your other housekeepers had lived in."

Justin growled. "That woman—"

"At least she's consistent," Sarah said. "I do have an idea, if you don't mind."

All serious now, Justin said, "Shoot."

"Mickie actually thought she was the only child who had ever been without a mom. I'm sure someone at church is in the same situation, but I know Bill was without his mom. If I contact Bill and we go over to see Marcy, since Mickie is so in love with her, it might help for her to let them share with her. And then there's a book, written on a child's level, about death and pain and going on with life. It's a real good book that subtly addresses those issues, if you wouldn't mind my picking it up for her."

Justin smiled, relieved. "Both ideas sound wonderful. I'll try to spend a little more time with her in the evening to fill in that loss she's experiencing."

"I don't know if it'll do any good. Mickie may just want a mommy, and it's something she's going to have to work through. Kids can be very stubborn sometimes."

"You're telling me."

"Hey, I've learned since I've been here." Sarah stood. "Don't worry about it. Pray, let God work it out. Who knows, maybe He wants Mickie to have a mommy and that was your wake-up call.'' She winked and left.

Justin sat at the table, dumbstruck at Sarah's words, until he heard her door click closed upstairs, then he stood and went up to bed, his mind still on the bombshell Sarah had dropped before leaving. Justin wondered if Sarah had any idea that he had been thinking along the same lines as Mickie these past two weeks.

He wondered what she'd do if she knew.

But since he wasn't going to tell her, it was a moot point.

''I'm surprised you're picking up Mickie today,'' the all-too-familiar voice said.

Lord, why me? Why is this woman becoming my thorn in the flesh?

''Why wouldn't I, Stephanie?'' Sarah asked mildly as she watched the last moments of the rehearsal. Other mothers were standing around waiting. She saw two fathers and a teenager, too.

''Well, after what happened at open house... Of course, we don't blame Mickie. I imagine it's all so confusing for her, having no mom and a woman living in the house like that.''

She made it sound so tawdry, Sarah thought, disgusted. ''Mickie has had other housekeepers,'' Sarah said, though she did admit that with her feelings for Justin she had been thinking more and more lately of moving out. Not only because the attraction was mutual, but because she was afraid she was going to end up hurting him. She had gone back and forth in her mind about the infertility issue. The fact was, she was absolutely terrified to mention it to him.

However, she knew she was going to have to do something, and Stephanie's words only reminded her of that.

"Well, I'm not one to gossip—"

Yeah, right, Sarah thought.

"But there were a couple of women at church the other day who were asking just who you were and why you always came to church with Justin. I tried to explain you were only the housekeeper, but I don't think they believed me."

Sarah smiled. "That's a shame. Sunday in church, why don't you introduce me. I'd like to meet them."

She walked off. Stephanie's simple jealousy was going to give Justin a bad name at church. She didn't know what to do. Since they were going to see Bill today, maybe she'd ask him if he had any ideas.

"I'm ready!" Mickie said, running up. "Are we still going to go see Bill today?"

Sarah smiled. "And Marcy."

"Great!" She jumped up and down, then took off toward the exit. She waited for Sarah at the door, then walked across the parking lot. As soon as she hit the grass, she ran to where the car was parked on the other side of the field.

Mickie rattled on about school and practice until they pulled into the driveway to Bill's place. Bill lived in a nice family house, one passed down through his father. She knew Bill had money but that he had never given up his job, insisting he was needed where he was.

Sarah wondered if he didn't sometimes resent his father's money and that was why he worked—to prove to everyone he could make it on his own. Still, Bill was a wonderful guy and had married a wonderful woman. She liked being around them both. He'd been her friend forever.

"Well, hello, pumpkin," Bill said, grinning and opening his arms to Mickie. She ran right into his hug.

"We got to come visit today because Aunt Sarah said so," Mickie announced, then squirmed out of his arms and raced toward Marcy.

Marcy knelt and hugged the little girl, then took her to the kitchen, where she cut up an apple and gave her a glass of milk. "Aunt Sarah says you don't have a mama, either," Mickie said to Bill as she munched the apple.

Bill chuckled. "Thank goodness we have such a forthright child. Why don't you and Marcy go look at that centerpiece you were going to borrow for Christmas dinner."

He sat down next to Mickie and smiled. "I guess that's just one more thing we have in common, isn't it, Mickie mine?"

Mickie, who had been swallowing a gulp of milk, set down the glass. Looking up, interested, she asked, "What else do we have in common?" She didn't comment on the nickname, just giggled.

"Well, we both had good daddies," he said, nodding at her with a grin.

Mickie smiled back. "Oh, yeah, my daddy's real good. He took me to the park the other day and tucks me in at night. Do you know, Nicole's dad never tucks her in? But my daddy does. Of course—" Mickie frowned "—her mama tucks her in."

She finished her snack and slid off the stool to play with the cat at her feet.

Bill knew Sarah had brought Mickie over for a reason. He had prayed about what to say. Watching Mickie now, he realized this was the first time he'd ever heard her talk about her mommy. "You miss her, don't you?" he said softly, picking up a box of treats and tossing one of the little cubes at the cat. The cat rolled over, holding it between its paws before biting down.

"Can I do that?" Mickie asked.

Bill tossed her a treat and she held it above the cat. She giggled when it sat up on its hind legs just like a dog, the way Bill had trained it to.

"Having a mommy must be the best thing in the world," Mickie finally said.

Bill shrugged. "My mom died when I was five. I missed her a lot. But I had my daddy."

"Jimmy told me I was the only one in the world without a mommy."

Bill shook his head. "Well, that's just not true. Many, many people don't have mommies. But tell me, what can a mommy do that a daddy can't?"

Mickie paused in stroking the cat, which was now curled contentedly in Mickie's lap, sniffing the box of treats as Mickie stroked her. "Make chocolate coconut cakes?"

Bill frowned, hard. "I dunno. Seems to me your daddy has made that cake once or twice for us."

Mickie nodded slowly. "Buy me dresses?"

Bill shook his head again. "I was with your daddy last year when he bought your Christmas present."

She fell silent for a long time. "Mommies can make daddies happy when daddies are alone," she finally said.

Bill was stunned. "Well, there you got me. But, honey," Bill said carefully, not wanting to hurt this little girl, "do you think your daddy is lonely?"

"Oh, no. He has me. That's just what Mrs. Winters said to a friend of hers. I just wish, sometimes, I had a mommy so she could go with me to plays and stuff, like the other kids."

Bill sighed. "Yeah, so did I. But my dad loved me. I was much luckier than others. At least I had a daddy."

Mickie looked confused. "If you didn't have a mommy, then you had to have a daddy, didn't you?"

Marcy and Sarah were coming into the room and Marcy was lugging a photo album. Bill was happy when Marcy spoke up.

"Oh, no, sweetheart. I didn't have a mommy or a daddy. I had several. My mommy and daddy both died when I was six years old. I had three different sets of parents raise me."

Mickie was intrigued. "What do you mean?"

Marcy sat down and for the next hour she and Mickie laughed over pictures of Marcy when she was a little girl. She told Mickie how she'd bought a camera with some money her first set of parents had given her. Then, when she moved from foster home to foster home, she took pictures. She did admit there was one foster home she didn't like, but that the third set of parents kept her until she moved out after she was grown.

Mickie was astonished, then happy when she realized other people besides her didn't have a mommy or a daddy. She was especially happy when Marcy mentioned someone at church who didn't have a mommy, a young girl she knew. Mickie told Marcy very solemnly that she would talk to Missy next week and explain that not everyone had mommies.

Sarah was satisfied with the day's events. But she wasn't surprised, when, after looking at the pictures, having another snack and finally preparing to leave, Mickie said, "But I still want a mommy."

What did surprise Sarah was when Mickie started her next sentence.

"I can't wait until Christmas because—" The little girl suddenly clamped a hand over her mouth.

Sarah stared quizzically at the child. "What Mickie?"

"Oh, no, Santa won't bring me what I ask for if I tell."

She stroked the cat again, then said, "I do wish I had a cat, though. Do you think Daddy might get me a cat?"

Sarah stared at Mickie. Was that what she had wished for? Oh, dear. She'd have to tell Justin because she was certain that wasn't on his Christmas list.

They started toward the door. Bill and Marcy escorted them out. But as Sarah started to get in the car, Bill stopped her. "Though you brought Mickie here today to talk, something is bothering you. Marcy mentioned you wanted to speak to me but said it could wait."

Now she knew what they'd been whispering about on the porch as she'd helped Mickie into the car. She shrugged. "I do have a problem and thought maybe to ask you about it."

Bill nodded. "I'm glad you came to me. Can you meet me for lunch tomorrow at the little restaurant near where Justin and I work?"

She knew which one he was talking about. He ate there all the time. Or he used to. She doubted he did much eating away from home since he'd married.

"Sure. It's nothing really serious," she said, her smile leaving her face as she thought about just what she'd wanted to discuss with Bill. "But if you're busy maybe I should—"

Bill took her shoulders. "You're like my sister, Sarah. When I didn't have anyone, you were there. I'm never too busy for you. If you'd only stop letting your pride get in the way when I offer help."

"But Marcy might not like—" she began, only to be cut off.

"Marcy knows you're nothing more than a friend to me. She loves you for what you did during our teenage years."

Sarah shrugged, feeling uncomfortable with the praise. "I didn't realize you'd ever told her how close we were. And I love Marcy dearly but was afraid she'd feel threatened by an unknown."

Bill chuckled. "We love each other too much for there to be any mistrust between us."

Sarah shook her head. "You're one of the lucky

few, then. Okay. I'll meet you around noon tomorrow."

He gave her a peck on the cheek, then waved to Mickie. Marcy was just coming down the steps after having gone back into the house to answer the phone. She hugged Sarah, too, and gave her a peck. "Take care, Mickie. And next time you see Jimmy, don't forget to tell him about the woman you met who had three mommies!"

Mickie giggled and waved bye.

Sarah got in the car and left. She could sigh in relief that she had accomplished two missions today.

First, Mickie knew she wasn't the only one in the world without a mommy. Sarah wasn't sure how much it would help. Maybe it would only open the door for Mickie to ask more questions, or maybe she would be satisfied completely. Still, it was a step forward.

And second, she had taken a step forward facing her fears about her infertility. She would talk to Bill and share with him the secret that she'd shared with no one except André. She would tell Bill what had really caused her breakup with André, tell him her fears and see how he reacted, then maybe she could figure out just how to tell Justin about her inability to have children.

She would decide if a relationship with him truly was a lost cause and she should just drift away, leaving him to find someone else to fill the empty space in his heart.

And she knew it was there. She'd glimpsed it in the short time they'd become closer. Oh, yes, Justin was just as lonely as she was. And if she wasn't wrong, she thought he might be seriously considering asking her to live happily ever after with him.

But *could* he be happy after her secret was discovered?

Chapter Eighteen

Sarah glanced around nervously, straightening the collar of her top, then smoothing her skirt.

"Relax, I'm sure Mickie's teacher has explained everything."

Sarah watched all the people mingling in the school auditorium, moving back and forth, finding seats, laughing, shaking hands, rushing children toward the back of the closed curtains on the dais. "Why did I come?" she asked, more to herself than anyone around her.

"Besides the fact that you're like me and obviously love to be embarrassed," Justin joked, then grinned, "you have a niece who would have been very upset if you hadn't shown up."

Sarah glanced up at Justin, who was in a pair of jeans and a pullover sweater, looking as if he hadn't a care in the world. "I'm sorry," she said in a low voice. "I didn't realize you'd be embarrassed, too."

Justin shrugged. "Not exactly embarrassed, just expecting some less-than-sensitive person to make a joke about what Mickie said.''

He urged her forward toward the fourth row, then motioned her toward the middle. "I'm worried about someone making a nasty comment," she replied, murmuring it for his ears only.

"No one will," he said, so certain.

"How can you be so sure?" She seated herself, noting a small crowd not too far away pointing, their heads together. Her cheeks turned pink.

"I'm intimidating, if nothing else," he replied, and took his seat beside her.

That caught her attention. "You *know* that?"

He chuckled and turned his warm gaze on her. "I've perfected it for business. One look can send troublemakers running."

She rolled her eyes and fell back against her seat. "I don't believe you. All this time I thought you didn't realize how you make people quake in their boots."

"They quake in their boots, do they?" he asked arrogantly.

She couldn't help but giggle. "You're incorrigible!"

"Maybe, but you're smiling now."

Seeing the glint in his eyes, she said, "You did that on purpose."

He shrugged.

Deciding it was wise to change the subject, she said, "So, is Mickie excited?"

Justin nodded. "She was dancing circles around the teacher when I dropped her off. She certainly has enough energy for the entire class tonight."

Sarah smiled softly. "I know. She made me try the costume on her each time I put another seam together. She had to watch its creation, step by step."

"That's Mickie. Do you know, at three years of age she asked me how the earth was made and how come, if the sun was a star, the other stars didn't have earths, too?"

Seeing the proud smile on his face, she realized he wasn't complaining at all. "She's something special."

"She sure is. I love her. My only regret is that she doesn't have a brother or sister."

Just like that, Sarah's smile collapsed. But she was saved from Justin's noting it by the dimming house-lights. Kids. Did that mean he wanted another one or that he *had,* at some time, wanted one when Mickie was younger? Maybe he thought he was too old now to have another baby. At least, she tried to tell herself that.

She felt his warm hand close over her smaller one and couldn't resist the touch. Justin was not only caus-ing her current conflict, he was also the very one who soothed it whenever she got too uptight.

Though he didn't know what was the matter, he always seemed to sense when something bothered her and found ways to put her at ease.

His hand felt good, warm, secure. She liked the feel of it. She didn't fight him but leaned closer, resting her arm against his and absorbing the heat from him, as if she could absorb his peace.

To a point it worked. The play started and she was able to relax as the children came out and sang an opening song. The play was about the shoemaker and the elves who came to help him make his shoes. Of course, it didn't follow the fairy tale exactly. Everyone had a lot of fun as the different shoes sang their songs of what Christmas was about. One pair, ballerina slippers, sang about the dancing at Christmas. Another pair, children's shoes, sang about favorite baby dolls that children liked. Then a pair of tennis shoes that belonged to a little boy sang about how bad he'd been and how he wouldn't get anything this Christmas. Through it all the adults laughed at the proper moments and cheered the different children. Only two small children forgot their lines.

Then it was Mickie's turn. The shopkeeper was at his lowest and angels appeared, singing the joys of Christmas.

"Doesn't she look great?" Justin whispered proudly as Mickie and the other children sang.

"Perfect," Sarah answered, just as quietly.

Then the elves were out fixing the shoes. Before long, the angels were singing again, then the shopkeeper gave the shoes to the owners and was able to save his shop after all.

The angels came back out for the final scene, and Sarah watched Justin's surprise and delight as Mickie sang a short solo. Her voice was loud and clear, and though she seemed scared when she first started, once she turned to her teacher and started singing, it went fine.

Justin looked as if he could pop buttons on his top he was so proud.

"Why didn't she tell me?" he asked.

Sarah grinned. "She wanted to surprise you."

"I didn't know she could keep a secret," he murmured, standing as the song finished and clapping along with everyone else.

Mickie came running out to where Justin and Sarah stood. "Are you proud, Daddy? Did I sing good?"

Justin swooped her up in his arms. "I'm very proud and you could make the angels sit up and take notice," he said, bussing her cheek. "How about I take you out for a chocolate sundae to show you how proud I am?"

"Oh, cool! And I can stay up late since there's no more school until after Christmas, can't I?"

"I suppose so," Justin said. "As long as you don't get cranky."

"Ice cream when it's cold outside?" Sarah asked.

Justin chuckled. "That's the best time."

They stopped at an ice-cream shop on the way home and Mickie enjoyed a sundae with Justin, while Sarah insisted she didn't want anything. She enjoyed watching the two decide on just what ice cream and toppings they wanted, arguing good-naturedly over what was the best, before they finally settled down at a table.

"I still can't believe you wouldn't have anything at all," Justin said, taking a bite of his sundae.

"Doesn't Aunt Sarah like ice cream?" Mickie whispered loudly to her daddy.

Justin turned to her, an eyebrow raised. "Is that the case? You don't like ice cream?"

She smiled. "I'd be cold for hours if I put that in me," she replied. "I do like it. But only in the summer."

"But, Aunt Sarah," Mickie said, "you just have to

put more blankets on your bed when you get home and you won't be cold."

Sarah rolled her eyes. "Why didn't I think of that?" she teased.

"In that case, you have to have one small taste," Justin said, dipping his spoon in his sundae and holding it out to her.

Sarah looked at the spoon, then at Justin's mouth, and flushed. Somehow, eating after him seemed so personal. And he knew it, if the innocent look he was giving her was any indication. She was never one to back down from a dare but there was always a first time. "I think...I'll pass this time, thanks," Sarah said quietly.

Justin hesitated a moment, then set the spoon back in his container. "Maybe that's wiser after all," Justin murmured, holding her gaze.

Then Mickie was done with her ice cream and ready to go. She noticed Justin had lost interest in his. The container was still almost full. He took it and dumped it in the garbage can.

They hurried through the biting wind to the car and in seconds were on their way home.

When they arrived, Sarah wasn't surprised to find Mickie had drifted off. "She's had a full day," she said softly, opening the door for Justin.

He motioned her inside. Closing the door behind him, he said, "But as you know, she's an early riser."

He headed upstairs and Sarah trailed along. Going to her drawers, she dug out Mickie's warm p.j.'s and handed them to Justin, who had already stripped off her shoes and socks. He lifted her and slipped the costume over her head, then pulled her top on.

Sarah folded back the sheets and added another blanket. "It's getting colder earlier this year," she whispered as Justin covered up Mickie.

He said a quick prayer over her, then kissed her and stood. Sarah added a kiss to Mickie's cheek, then left the room. Justin pulled the door closed behind him.

Then they both stood there staring at each other. Sarah had enjoyed the companionship tonight, the feel of another human next to her, the joy of sharing a joke. She hated for it to end.

Evidently, so did Justin. "You want some cocoa before you go to bed?"

Sarah's eyes widened. She opened her mouth to say yes, but he must have thought otherwise, for he added, "You did say you'd have trouble warming up."

She chuckled, her mouth spreading into a smile. "I'd love some. But why don't you let me make it."

He nodded. They walked down the stairs together and she went into the kitchen, where she quickly made up some cocoa. Coming back out, she found Justin, his hands in his jean pockets, standing before the blinking Christmas tree, staring thoughtfully at it.

The whole room looked like Christmas with the tree blinking, the silver icicles waving gently from the air blowing out of the overhead ducts. Greenery with gold and red was draped across everything. Stockings were suspended from the mantel. And mistletoe hung from the fan in the middle of the living room.

The room had a very homey feeling, one she was proud of, since she'd done most of the decorating.

"This is the best the house has looked since before Amy died," Justin said, turning from the tree and coming over to take his cocoa. He seated himself by Sarah on the couch.

Sarah took a sip of her cocoa, continuing to stare at the tree despite Justin's presence next to her on the right or the fireplace on the left. She kicked off her shoes and folded one foot under her, then slipped the other one up on the coffee table. "Everything was in the attic, Justin. All you had to do was pull it down and put it up."

Justin shrugged. "When Amy died, some of the magic died, too, I suppose. I had no desire or wish to celebrate an all-out humdinger of a Christmas again." He took a sip of his cocoa, then said, "But I'd forgotten what I was missing. What *Mickie* was missing."

Sarah wrapped her hands around her mug. "No wishes?" she asked, thinking of all the wishes she'd had that Christmas.

"No happy ones," he said, echoing her feelings. "They were all tainted with my dark thoughts over all the grief Mickie and I were experiencing."

He shifted his body, which brought him closer, though she doubted he realized it, staring as intently as he was at the blinking lights. "But that's what I was doing just now—thinking about Christmas wishes. Christmas has always been considered a time for kids, but I've always made my own Christmas wishes, too. After all, wasn't that when we received the greatest gift? It reminds us that there is such a thing as happiness and goodness and the chance for things to turn out right in the end.''

Sarah nodded. ''I agree. It should be a time of hope and joy, and a time to remember that Amy's in a better place.''

Justin sank back into the cushions of the couch. ''That was the conclusion I came to last year. I guess that's why this year it has been easier during the holidays and we've done so much better.''

He took another sip of his cocoa, then turned toward Sarah. ''So tell me, what is your Christmas wish this year?''

The crackling of the flames from the fire Justin had started while she was in the kitchen was the only sound in the room. She looked into Justin's deep brown eyes and wanted to tell him, *You. I want you for Christmas.* But since that wasn't appropriate—she could just imagine her mother rolling over in her grave if she said that—she said, instead, ''I don't know. Maybe a family.''

She saw him set his cup down and she felt the air around them change.

''But you have us, Sarah.''

She nodded. Oh, dear. Her and her big mouth. She couldn't explain that she wanted a baby to hold, couldn't tell him about the pain inside her heart. But the pain wasn't as bad if she thought of Mickie as partly hers. No, she couldn't say that, so instead she asked him, ''And you? What do you want for Christmas? What are your wishes?''

Justin turned his gaze back to the tree, which relieved Sarah. He was too perceptive and she'd just known he was going to see something she hadn't wanted him to. She studied his masculine jaw, the hint of shadow his gold whiskers caused. Short light lashes didn't move as he stared hard at the tree.

"Earlier in the year I might have said the only wish I had was for my favorite little girl to be happy." A ghost of a smile touched his lips. "Mickie is already a very happy girl, though. Still, I'd like to erase the loneliness in her eyes sometimes. Of course, I could've also wished business were better, but it's going really good." The smiled widened and he turned, his eyes touching hers. "I could also wish for a normal tie that didn't have some sort of cartoon or fish or even flower on it."

Sarah laughed, but the laughter was strained because the look on his face had just turned serious.

"But things have changed," he said. "If I had to ask Santa now, it'd be for a warm, loving woman who could love me in return."

Her mouth fell open. Her breath lodged in her chest. She couldn't comment for anything in the world.

And she didn't have to. Justin, taking her quiet as a signal for him to continue, pulled her gently into his arms and lowered his lips to hers.

I could love you, she thought fleetingly as his warm, tender lips, expertly wrung a response from her. *I do love you.*

She had been wanting, for more than an hour, for him to kiss her. The kiss was brief and achingly tender. Her heart was racing and her fingers tingling when he pulled back. She opened heavy eyelids to see Justin gazing down at her.

''You know any women like that?'' he asked huskily.

Sarah stared at him a moment, trying to figure out what he was talking about. When she realized he was asking her if she loved him in return, her gaze slid away. ''It's not that easy,'' she said, trying to hide the pain. Did he really mean he loved her and was serious about her? Her heart thudded in her chest.

''Yes, Sarah, it is. It's that easy. All you have to say is yes.''

Oh, no! No! No! No! It wasn't that easy at all. Her chest felt as if it were going to explode with the pain of what she needed to tell him. *Why didn't you tell him before this?* Because she hadn't known this was coming. What could she say? She knew what she wanted to say. But fairy tales were just that. Fairy tales. Make-believe. They didn't come true. ''Can you give me some time?'' she asked hesitantly, not wanting to see the hurt in his eyes.

But she felt it. He stiffened and pulled back. ''Of course I can, Sarah. I'd never pressure any woman for an answer like that.''

She'd ruined the night. That sweet sharing spirit was gone, replaced by one of formality. As if to prove her point, Justin changed the subject.

''I wanted to let you know there are two openings at my business that I think you're qualified for.''

She turned shocked eyes on him. Surely he wasn't that upset.

''It's not what you're thinking. I said I'd give you time to think, and I will. But just because I'm giving you time doesn't mean I won't stop wanting a relationship with you.''

This time Sarah's eyes widened with comprehension. He really did care for her, really did have serious feelings for her....

"However, I think it's time that we changed the living and working arrangements. I don't want you to feel pressured or feel uncomfortable. We both know that despite our feelings nothing improper has gone on here. But people like Stephanie Williams may start gossip. I want to protect you from that sort of thing,'' he added.

She nodded. "Fine. Okay.'' She stood.

Justin turned his gaze back toward the Christmas tree, and though she knew he was amused at her reaction, she could still see the sadness in his eyes. "If you'll excuse me, I'll clean up the cups tomorrow. I think I should just go to bed.''

Justin nodded. "Good idea, Sarah mine. Go to sleep and dream of tonight. Let me know when you're ready to talk again.''

Knees knocking, she almost ran up the stairs. She wondered what he thought her reasons were for not answering. Surely he realized she was just as attracted to him, that she had fallen head over heels in love with the kind, generous, loving person he was. She could easily live happily ever after with him.

But of course he wouldn't know that, nor would he know it was he who would be having second thoughts when she finally told him the reason she had avoided answering him: she had to give him a chance to turn her down after he heard about her problem.

And she would make sure to go talk to Bill tomorrow. Maybe he would have a suggestion on how to tell Justin about her affliction without his being hurt or feeling used.

Please, Father, help me, she whispered, going into her room. *Please help me find a way to keep from hurting him. I've waited too long already and all I can now see is pain in the future.*

Chapter Nineteen

"Over here."

Sarah glanced across the lunch crowd to where Bill was seated. She waved and crossed to him. "Boy, I'd forgotten how busy this place is. It's been an eternity since I've been here."

Bill pulled out her chair and she rolled her eyes.

"So, what'll you have?" he asked as the waitress walked up.

Sarah thought about not ordering anything. She'd been a nervous wreck since talking with Justin the night before. But she knew Bill wouldn't let her get away without eating. "Soup, salad and sandwich of the day," she said to the waitress. "And ice water."

Bill ordered the same, and in no time at all the waitress was back with their salad. Bill devoured half of his before pushing it away and starting his quiz. "So, you wanna tell me what was eating at you when you were over at the house?"

Sarah swallowed a bite of salad, feeling that it was

a lump of coal instead of a tasty ranch-dressing-coated piece of lettuce. "I enjoy my job," she started, wondering now if she should really discuss this with Bill. She loved Justin. It was him she should be telling, not Bill.

But Bill couldn't hurt her the way Justin could, she realized.

"I'm not blind. Your job isn't the only thing you enjoy there, either," he said bluntly. "Tell me, what's bothering you."

"You're always so impatient," she grouched. She nodded toward her salad when the waitress came back, indicating she was done, then accepted the soup. "I was furious, humiliated, upset and a whole other list of things when André left."

"I know. I remember your shock over his actions. I still can't believe he just walked away and mailed you a letter."

"It wasn't exactly like that," Sarah said, remembering she hadn't told Bill everything.

Bill paused in taking a sip of soup. He raised an eyebrow. "And just how was it?" he asked pointedly.

"Don't get that look with me, Bill. You may be like a brother to me, but that doesn't mean I have to tell you everything. You were engaged at the time, remember?"

He nodded, a wary expression on his face. "And?"

"Well, remember the surgery I had a few months ago?"

"For the tumor on your ovaries? Yes?"

"I didn't tell you everything the doctor said. Unfortunately, I didn't think it would be a problem, until I met André.''

Sarah laid down her spoon. The helplessness and rage boiled up again. Why, oh, why, had she lost almost all of her ovaries. ''The doctor said that with only a quarter of one ovary left I'd likely never have babies.''

Only silence met that statement. She couldn't look up at Bill and see the same disgust or even pity that might be on his face. But when he reached over and touched her hand, she couldn't help but cast a glance at him. Only pain registered in his eyes. Surprised, she kept her gaze on his.

''And that's why André left?'' he asked.

Sarah felt tears brim in her eyes. ''Yes. He said he needed time and took a vacation, but then he had his father get rid of me. I can't explain the pain. I felt so inadequate as a woman, so angry at myself because I was useless.''

''Sarah, no. You aren't useless.''

''Oh, yeah, I know that here.'' She touched her head. ''But not here.'' She touched her heart. ''Or here.'' She touched her abdomen. ''I'd always wanted kids. I thought André would adopt. I mean, true, I was devastated. I didn't realize how important it was to him or his family that their line be carried on. I guess I should have. Every man wants a boy to carry on the family name.''

''Adoption would carry on the name.''

''But not the bloodline.''

Bill's hands fisted and he said something under his breath. Sarah didn't want to know. ''Don't be angry,

Bill. It's over and done with. And don't pity me. I've accepted it, sort of.''

The waitress brought their sandwiches and they began to eat. Bill had gotten through half of his before he'd calmed down enough to resume the conversation. ''What did you want to see me for, then?''

''It's about Justin.''

''Has he done the same thing?'' Bill demanded, his face beginning to turn red with outrage.

''No!'' Sarah said, dropping her sandwich. She toyed with it for a moment before looking up at Bill. ''He doesn't know.''

''You're serious about him,'' he said, satisfied. Then he frowned. ''Just how serious?''

''Very serious.''

Bill whistled. ''And you haven't told him?''

Sarah shook her head. ''I kept putting it off because I was so embarrassed. After all, there was nothing really going on between us, so there was no need for him to know.''

Bill nodded. ''I can understand your reasoning. Then it got serious and you couldn't just blurt it out.''

''That's right,'' she said, relieved he wasn't going to condemn her.

''He asked me last night if I could love him. Oh, Bill, I want to say yes, but I know he'll think I was hiding this from him. I don't want to hurt him. He's so good with kids. You know, he told me he regretted not giving Mickie a brother.''

Bill reached out and took her hand. ''But if you love him, Sarah, you have to tell him and leave the decision up to him.''

She nodded, blinking back her tears. "I know that. I just don't know how. How do you say, 'oh, by the way, I'm infertile and I know you want more kids, but you're gonna have to pick between the two'?"

Bill frowned, then asked, "How'd you tell André?"

She laughed bitterly. "That was easy. One night he asked me if I wanted kids. Thinking he didn't really want them, I said I was infertile so it didn't matter."

Bill winced.

"Exactly. Imagine my surprise when he asked me what had given me the idea he didn't want kids. Then he said it was expected that the family bloodline be carried on through him. And all the time I'd thought he was different from his parents."

"Justin isn't like that."

"But I just can't ask him to pick," she whispered.

"That's his right, Sarah. Unless you can read his mind, you don't know what he wants."

"Just like André, huh," she said, resigned.

"Yeah. Give Justin a chance."

"But how?" she asked. "I've gone over this a million times. How do I go about telling him? What if he has questions? How can I stand there in front of him and give him all these answers without my emotions taking over?"

Bill now toyed with his sandwich instead of eating it. Bill never toyed with his food. That just went to show how touchy this subject was to a man.

Finally, Bill's face brightened. "Do you have a copy of your doctor's reports?"

"No. I never thought I could get them."

"Of course you can. Here's what you do. Use my

phone,'' he said, digging out his cell phone. ''Call your doctor. Tell him you're on your way over for copies of his reports. Get the copies, then highlight any pertinent information. Outline your speech, just as lawyers do when they're working up a case, then present the argument to Justin. You can hand him the report copies and tell him he can read them over if he has any questions.''

Sarah brightened, too, feeling a burden lift from her shoulders. ''You know, that just might work. If I have everything in front of me to show him, it might actually give me the courage to go through with this. At least then, when he backs off, I'll know it wasn't my fault because I bungled the telling, as with André.''

She dialed her doctor's number.

''André isn't like Justin,'' Bill said. ''Besides, I doubt you'll get through the speech before Justin sweeps you into his arms and tells you it doesn't matter.''

Sarah spoke into the receiver to the nurse who'd answered the phone, before responding to Bill. ''I only wish it wouldn't matter. But think how you'd feel if this were Marcy,'' she said.

''I am,'' he said softly just as Sarah turned her attention back to the phone and set up a time to pick up the records.

''I can go right over,'' she said, handing Bill the phone back. She looked at him and her distress must have shown, because he reached out and took her hand.

''Sarah, he might be upset, but it'll be for your benefit, not his. If he loves you, that's all that'll matter.''

"But it didn't to André."

"He didn't love you," Bill replied. "Besides, he's weak. Justin isn't. Would a weak man go back to a family who had been wronged by his partner and offer recompense for his wrongs?"

Fresh tears filled her eyes. "You're right. What a fool I've been." She stood and hugged Bill. "I've got to go." She took out some money and tossed it on the table. "Don't argue," she warned when he opened his mouth. "You can treat me next time. And don't mention this conversation to anyone until I get back and tell you the outcome."

She headed toward the door, excitement making her steps bounce.

"Was that Sarah?"

Bill turned to see Justin walking up. "Yeah. We had lunch today. What brings you here?"

Justin seated himself across from Bill. "I called your office and they told me you were here."

Bill was thankful Justin hadn't shown up any earlier. Sarah would have found her plans to confide in Bill destroyed. She might not have had the ability to tell Justin everything as calmly and logically as she would now with her confidence restored. Bill didn't say that; instead, he merely nodded. "So, what's up?"

Justin ordered coffee, then turned to Bill. "Sarah is."

Bill raised his eyebrows. "What do you mean by that?"

"I hesitate to tell you just after finding you here with Sarah."

Bill chuckled. "I don't break confidences. But if

you don't want to talk about her, then let me tell you about Marcy.''

"I asked Sarah if she loves me."

Oh, well, so much for his not wanting to confide in Bill. Bill didn't think Justin had even heard his comment about Marcy.

Justin sipped his coffee and played with the sugar holder. "Well, I didn't exactly phrase it that way. I never would have thought I'd say that to anyone again. But Sarah has a way of getting under your skin. I mean, I did hire her simply because I needed a sitter and wanted to prove to her I bore her no ill will. But I didn't expect this.''

Oh, yeah, his buddy had it bad. And he couldn't be more thrilled. Unlike Sarah, Bill didn't think it would make a huge difference to Justin that Sarah probably couldn't have children. No, Justin just wanted to find someone who would love him and love his little girl. No one could fill that bill better than Sarah. "So, what did you expect?'' Bill asked, amused at the way his friend was fighting his feelings. He did feel just a little sorry for him, but he'd have tons of teasing material after Justin and Sarah were married.

"I don't know. I didn't know from the first day she showed up on my doorstep what to expect. It's like I've been sucked into a tornado. My common sense went on vacation and I've been operating solely on emotions ever since.''

Bill chuckled. "Is that so bad?''

Justin grinned, but it was a self-deprecating grin. "I never dreamed I'd want home and hearth with a woman again, want to go shopping with her, see her carrying my child, watch her when she's cooking or outside pruning the roses.''

Bill frowned at Justin's words. "Well, what if she can't cook or hates roses or doesn't want kids?''

Justin shrugged. "Sarah can cook, likes roses *and* kids.''

"There's a difference between liking kids and wanting kids.''

Again Justin shrugged. "That can be worked through. I just want her love.'' He frowned then. "But she wants time. I know I'm being crazy, but I'm wondering if maybe she doesn't feel obligated or something and that's why she wants time, to work herself up into accepting my proposal.''

"Sarah's not like that,'' Bill said. "I'd bet she loves you, too.'' It was as close as he could come without breaking his word to Sarah—something he wouldn't do, no matter how much he wanted to at the moment.

Justin still didn't look convinced, so Bill added, "Give her time. She'll open up. Why else would she be marrying, if not for love?''

"So, how'd you get so wise?'' Justin asked, joking.

Bill spread his arms. "Marcy fell into my arms with no problems, so I must be wise.''

Justin only laughed.

And though Bill laughed with him, he felt the first inkling of unease. Could Sarah have been right to worry about Justin's reactions? Sarah had seemed so sure that Justin would be upset. And it was only now that Bill was finally realizing that Justin might actually not trust another female after the way Amy had hurt him.

He said a quick prayer that God would work everything out according to His will.

Chapter Twenty

"Daddy, do you love Aunt Sarah?"

Justin almost ran off the road.

"Wh-what did you ask, honey?" he sputtered. Kids always saw everything, he supposed, chastising himself for not hiding his feelings better.

"I love Aunt Sarah. She's really nice. I just wondered if you love her, too."

"Well, it's sorta hard to explain," he said, then glanced over and saw his daughter's guileless look. "Yes, honey, I love Aunt Sarah. She's very nice. But you have to remember, adult love is different. I mean, there's more than just love to consider—"

He broke off and shook his head. Mickie wouldn't understand what he was trying to say, when he himself didn't understand what it was. Besides, she was grinning and looking at something she saw out the window. She didn't need to hear his fears. He'd admitted to Mickie he cared for Sarah. What would Mickie understand besides that?

A lot, he thought warily, looking again to see if she was going to bring up the subject. When she didn't, he realized a weight had lifted off him. He'd been wondering how to break his feelings to Mickie and just when to tell her. She acted as though it didn't matter at all. Maybe that meant it wouldn't matter if he and Sarah decided to marry. After all, Mickie had told everyone at school Aunt Sarah was her mom. Of course, lying about it and actually allowing someone else into his life were two different things.

Getting remarried was just too much for any one person to handle. He wondered how people managed the stress. Which made him wonder again why Sarah had been so hesitant to return his love. Oh, she enjoyed his kisses and embraces. They had a wonderful time together. And he saw something in her eyes that he'd never seen in his wife's. Or was it his imagination? Did he really see a tenderness and yearning in Sarah, a desire to be with him always?

Suddenly aware of how much he wanted to see something special in Sarah's eyes made him realize he'd made the right decision to bring home those applications. She was becoming too much of a temptation and he wouldn't dare do anything that would hurt his daughter or Sarah's reputation—or his soul.

"Look! Mrs. Winters is home!"

Justin had just pulled into his driveway, and he saw Mrs. Winters unloading her car. Relieved, he realized he could get Sarah out of the house quickly now. Maybe that was the problem. She was afraid to admit to him she cared for him because she was still living in the house. It would be much harder on them both if she admitted it while still living there. The temptation would be too great.

Getting out of the car, he allowed Mickie to go over and say hi to one of her favorite neighbors.

"Well, hi there, Mickie. How have you been doing?"

"Great! Did you know my aunt Sarah is living with us now?"

Mrs. Winters chuckled. "Is that so? You like her as your baby-sitter, do you?"

"Yeah, but she can't cook as good as you. But that's okay. Sometimes she cooks really, *really* good."

Mrs. Winters chuckled again and turned to Justin. "I was going to come over later to let you know I was home. Whenever you needed me to baby-sit, I'll be here."

Mickie frowned and turned to her daddy. "We won't need her if Aunt Sarah is here, will we, Daddy?"

Justin laughed. "Well, pumpkin, Aunt Sarah may be getting another job and leaving temporarily."

Seeing the fear in her eyes, he added, "But she'll be visiting you just about every day."

"But you love her," Mickie said.

Justin flushed under Mrs. Winters's knowing look. Maybe he shouldn't have told his daughter that, he thought wryly. He simply shrugged at Mrs. Winters. "Sometimes, pumpkin, that's why you have to move out. It's better since we aren't married yet."

Realizing that he'd accidentally added "yet," he flushed in earnest. He wasn't one to let something slip like that and he didn't like that he'd done it in front of someone other than Sarah. "You'll move out one day, honey," Justin said, trying to cover his mistake, hoping Mickie wouldn't realize what he'd said.

"Never, Daddy. I'll always live with you."

When she didn't say anything else, he breathed a small sigh of relief. Things were just too good right now. He was lucky Mickie hadn't caught his mistake and advertised it to the entire neighborhood. Turning back to Mrs. Winters, he said, "You'll have to come over and meet Sarah before she leaves. Maybe for supper one night. Let me speak to her first."

"Of course," Mrs. Winters replied, and headed toward her door. "Take care of that daddy of yours, Mickie."

"I will," she said, and crossed the street holding her daddy's hand.

"Well now, if you're gonna take care of me, then don't you tell Sarah about the gifts we shopped for. Just go find her and tell her I'm home for lunch."

"Okay!" Mickie said, and started up the stairs.

Sarah stared down at the pile of papers on the small writing desk. On top of them lay a clean sheet of computer paper with the words *To Do:*

Underneath she wrote:

1. Tell Justin I'm infertile.
2. Tumors discovered during annual Pap. Only one-quarter of an ovary left.
3. Why André dumped me...

No! she thought, and drew a line through the phrase.

3. Doesn't deserve half a wife.
4. But I love him.
5. Give him doctor's reports and tell him he can have time to read them.

Loud steps sounded on the stairs and Sarah realized Mickie and her daddy were home. Quickly, she shoved all the papers in the top drawer. Mickie was a dear, but she would question her to death if she caught her writing.

"Guess what?" Mickie said, running in. "Mrs. Winters is back and we bought Christmas presents and Daddy says you'll move out, probably until you marry him, and he's only going to be home for lunch today and you need to come fix it for him—can I go to the next-door neighbors' since I've already eaten?"

Sarah blinked. Then she nodded. "But, Mickie," she said as Mickie turned to run out the door, "don't be telling anyone else what you told me, okay?"

Mickie shrugged and was out the door. Sarah realized she hadn't made a bit of sense, but how could she have when she'd suddenly found out Justin was talking to his daughter about her and Justin getting married. And she hadn't even had her talk with him yet!

Going down the stairs, she caught Justin just as he was coming into the living room. Swallowing her fear, she said, "I need to speak with you."

When she realized she'd left her notes upstairs she started to turn. Justin's smile stopped her.

"I want to talk to you, too." He caught her hand. "Come in here."

The phone rang, stopping him, for which she was thankful. She turned once again to go get her notes. That was when she saw Justin's face darken.

Looking up at her, he said, "Can you hold this until I go into the other room?"

She nodded and went over to where Justin stood. Lifting the phone to her ear, she planned to wait until she heard the click of the extension. She was distracted when Mickie came barreling down the stairs with her doll. Sarah covered the receiver and asked Mickie to close the door.

When she lifted the receiver back to her ear, she got the shock of her life.

"Okay, Drydan, what do you want?"

Drydan Watson was on the line. Her stomach dropped to her toes and she felt ill. *Put the phone down. You're invading his privacy,* her mind screamed, but her heart kept the phone to her ear.

"I want bygones to be bygones. My son is back in town and I finally found out what was going on between those two."

"This really isn't any of my business, Drydan."

"But it is when she's tried to ruin my reputation. You see, my son found out she was infertile and trying to marry him for his money...."

The sound of a car door penetrated Sarah's hypnotic haze and she lowered the phone. She stood staring at the receiver, dizzy with pain. She had wanted to tell Justin. Drydan would make her sound guilty. She knew how manipulative he was.

She had to tell Justin her side of the story.

Panic gripped her heart and she forced herself to

take first one step, then another, toward the library. She would go in there, explain that Drydan was a liar, tell Justin everything: that she was infertile—or at least, they were ninety-nine percent certain. No, she would be honest. There was no way she could have kids. The chances were less than a million to one, as far as her doctor was concerned. She would tell Justin that and explain that she was just afraid.

Her heart beat loudly in her ears, sounding like someone pounding on wood.

Sarah's head whipped around. No, someone *was* knocking. She hadn't been able to distinguish the sound over her own thudding heart.

Who in the world could it be? Now, right when everything was caving in on her, who could be knocking at her door?

She hesitated, thought not to answer it, but then, feeling her courage drain in the face of what Drydan had had time to tell Justin, she turned and ran to the door as if she'd been tossed a lifeline. Maybe it was Bill. Maybe it was Marcy or maybe...

"Oh, no... It can't be!" she whispered when she opened the door. She grabbed the wooden structure for support and gripped it as her knees gave out.

"Sarah? We need to talk."

André stood there, his hair ruffled from the breeze, a look of seriousness in his eyes that boded ill will.

Chapter Twenty-One

"May I come in?"

Sarah swallowed hard. "Yes."

When she just stood there, André took her elbow and escorted her to the couch. Sarah's mind was numb. All she could think was that Justin was in one room talking to Drydan and her whole present was about to fall apart, while André had just shown up at her door to rehash the past.

"Sarah. Did you hear me?"

"Huh?" she focused on André. Dear, gorgeous André, who had his whole life ahead of him now that he'd gotten rid of his little problem. Namely her.

"I said, I can't believe what my father did. I meant what I said when I told you I was taking some time off to think. My father had no authority to have you fired. You were my legal assistant. He took too much upon himself."

Forcing herself to concentrate on André, she was surprised by his words. "Look, André, you were dumping me. What did it matter?'' All she wanted was to get to Justin and explain.

"Dumping you?" André shook his head, shock evident on his face. "Sarah, I told you I needed time to think. That's what I did. My father is the one who was behind the rest.''

Sarah didn't understand, but he certainly had her attention. "What are you trying to say, André?"

"I love you. I still want to marry you. Look, I know my parents put you through the ringer, and I've had a long talk with them. They won't interfere again. I was especially furious when my father told me you were working as a housekeeper! A housekeeper, with your experience.''

"Well, it wasn't as if I could get a reference from your father," she said sarcastically, her pain and anger coming out against this man.

"No. And for that I'm sorry. Why didn't you call me? I left my number with…"

His voice trailed off and she couldn't resist asking, "Your father?"

He sighed and rubbed a hand down his face. "Yes, my father." He growled. "I've been an idiot. I thought I needed time alone and found all I could think of was you. Only you.''

He stood and began to pace, pushing his coat back so he could slide his hands into his pockets. "It doesn't matter if we have children or not. I've let my father dictate my life too long. It's you I want. I understand you were hurt and didn't have anywhere to go and your ex-brother-in-law took you in. I just hope he hasn't taken advantage of the situation.''

"André!" Sarah said, shocked.

André turned back to her. "I didn't mean that. I'm still upset over the fight I just had with my dad. Can't you understand? I love you. I want you back. Are you planning to work here the rest of your life?"

Sarah thought of the applications Justin was supposed to bring her. "No, André," she said wearily. "I don't plan on staying a housekeeper."

"Good. I'm setting up my own practice. I want you to work for me. You won't have to worry about my father again. What do you say?"

"That sounds like a good idea, Sarah. Maybe you ought to consider it."

"Justin?" She whirled around to find him standing near the foot of the stairs at the entrance to the side hallway.

He sauntered into the room. His features were masked, but there was something roiling in his gaze. Anger? Disillusionment? Hurt? Pain? "I said André has offered you everything back. Sounds too good to pass up. You ought to consider it."

Just like that her hope died. Justin had talked to Drydan and Drydan had carried through on his threat. He had told Justin about her infertility, plus who knew what else. And Justin saw this as the perfect way to get rid of her. She wouldn't have believed it of him.

Of course, she didn't have any right to be upset. She'd told herself she'd give him the right to choose. And he chose a better life for his daughter than her being an only child.

She was glad for the numbness right now. It would help her deal with everything. But later—oh, yes, later—she would grieve what she was losing. Because she realized she didn't love André at all. No, it was Justin she loved—deeply. And she doubted she would ever love anyone again as much as she loved Justin.

Forcing herself to swallow, she nodded. "Thank you, Justin. If you don't mind, I'll leave now."

"You don't have anywhere to live," Justin reminded her.

"I'll see she has a place," André said, not unkindly. "You can't expect me to allow her to continue to work as a housekeeper here, though."

"No, I don't suppose I'd like it, either," Justin said.

Sarah noted the way the two men talked over her. Normally, she would be spitting mad, but she still didn't feel anything.

"I'll send someone for my things," she said, and without looking back walked to the door. "Tell Mickie—" the pain in her heart broke through the numbness and she gasped "—tell her goodbye."

"Sarah…" Justin said.

But she didn't stop. She felt André's hand on her, escorting her to his car. She was grateful.

"I'll take you to my house and—"

"Take me to Bill's."

"Now, Sarah," he began.

"Take me there or I'll walk."

"As you wish," André said reluctantly.

Sarah laid back her head and closed her eyes. Only then did she finally allow the pain to engulf her, and the tears to silently flow down her face.

* * *

"What a fool," Justin berated himself, going back
into his office and sinking into his chair. "Why did
you let her go like that?"

But Justin knew. Oh, it wasn't because of what Drydan had said.

He knew that Drydan had not told him the truth.
Sarah wasn't a manipulative person who tried to marry
André for his money.

No, Sarah had loved André. And for some reason,
André had left her. Probably because he'd found out
she was infertile.

Justin wondered if Sarah had planned to tell him.
He was still reeling over that. Why hadn't she told
him? Was she worried he'd be angry? Or maybe she
was worried he'd kick her out? After all, he'd taken
her in off the streets.

But he wouldn't have done anything like that, because he loved her.

He'd gone out to confront her, and had heard André
saying his father had been behind everything.

It was then that he realized why Sarah hadn't been
able to voice her love for him. She was still in love
with André. And knowing Sarah as he now did, he
understood that she wouldn't have told him, would
feel guilty for leading him on.

It had broken his heart to know she was coming to
him just as Amy had.

But he wouldn't let her do it. Not just for him and
Mickie, but for her, too. That's why he'd told her she
might want to try going back to André.

And she hadn't even put up a fuss; she'd jumped at
the idea.

He'd thought he hurt when Amy died, but he knew he was hurting again—a wound he wasn't sure he would get over this time.

He scrubbed at his eyes, trying to erase the images his mind conjured up of Sarah. But it was no use. She was there, would be there—

"Daddy, where did Aunt Sarah go?"

Justin's head shot up.

Mickie was standing in the doorway, holding her doll, staring at him uncertainly.

What could he tell Mickie? How could he tell her?

"She moved out, honey," he said.

"Moved out? But she didn't tell me goodbye. She promised she'd always tell me goodbye."

Justin didn't know what to say. Angry at Sarah and himself for putting his daughter through this, he vowed never again to get involved with a woman. He held out his arms. "I'm sorry, pumpkin."

In a flash she was across the floor and climbing into his arms. Little sobs shook her body, and he rocked her, his own tears silently falling down his face. Why, oh, why, had he allowed the woman such a place in his heart?

He didn't realize his daughter had stopped crying or that it had gotten dark out. He did feel the touch of her small hand on his cheek and hear her whispered words.

"It's all right, Daddy. She'll come back. Don't you worry."

Looking down at the small child who was trying to comfort him, he hugged her close. Kissing the top of her head, he said, "What say we go make a chocolate coconut cake with extra coconut?"

''That sounds good,'' she said. But though she replied positively, her little eyes were far too serious.

Justin realized then that he'd have to push Sarah from his mind and concentrate, instead, on the life he had right in front of him. In time, he and Mickie would heal. Someday they'd be happy again.

Wouldn't they?

Chapter Twenty-Two

"Sarah, it's Bill."

Sarah glanced toward the front door of the garage apartment Bill had leased to her. Bill had pushed open the door and was peeking inside. Seeing him, his head covered with snowflakes, she motioned to him. "Come in," she said. "I was just finishing up my résumé for the job I'm applying for Monday."

"Marcy sent me over. It's Christmas Eve. She wanted to know if you'd come over and share dinner with us."

Christmas Eve? Already. An entire week had passed and she hadn't realized it. In another way, it seemed that an entire lifetime had passed since she'd walked out of Justin's life. "I don't know, Bill. I have so much to do—"

"May I ask you a question?" Bill sat down on the couch across the room from where Sarah sat at the table.

Sarah avoided his gaze and went back to typing.

"Sure. Shoot. After all, you rented me this place without any questions. I'm sure you're entitled to a few."

She knew that was a low blow, but she really didn't want him asking questions.

"Good try, Sarah," he said. "But I don't run when you get nasty."

"I'm sorry, Bill," she said, and looked up at him, only to see his compassionate gaze. "Don't," she warned.

"You're gonna drive yourself into a grave. Every time I glance over here I see the light on. You've done more this past week than anyone should do in a month. You need to slow down."

"I'm just trying to find a job."

"If that's so, why didn't you take the one Justin offered?"

She stiffened.

"I see," he said at last when she didn't comment. "What happened, Sarah? I don't understand why you're here. Justin loves you."

"Yeah, sure," she finally said, bitterness slipping into her voice.

Bill looked surprised but said, "So it is Justin. I'd wondered."

"Bill, don't bring it up. Please."

He ignored her. After going over to where she sat, he forced her around and took her hands. "I don't know what happened, Sarah. But I do know one thing. Justin loves you. Whatever's the matter can be worked out. You've got to try." When she didn't comment, he asked, "Does this have to do with what you told him—that you were infertile?"

Sarah tried to run away, but he wouldn't let her. "Does it? Are you telling me he went crazy over that? Well?"

She struggled against his hold, then stopped fighting. Her voice a broken whisper, she finally admitted, "I never got the chance to tell him."

Bill stared at her for only a minute, then let go of her hands and took a seat next to her. "Then what is all this about?"

Tears brimming her eyes, Sarah said, "I didn't get a chance to tell him because Drydan did."

He shook his head. "Wait a minute. You want to run that by me again? You said nothing about Drydan going over there that day."

Sarah sighed and dropped her head to her chest, her shoulders feeling heavy with the truth of that day. Finally, she said, "You remember your advice about notes? Well, I did it. I'd decided to confess everything. I went downstairs, planning on just that. But when I got down there, the phone rang. Drydan was on the line. He told Justin all kinds of things. Enough that when Justin came out he sent me home with André."

"Why didn't you try to tell him that what Drydan said was wrong?"

Sarah looked up helplessly. "I don't know. André was telling me he still loved me. Justin was telling me it'd be best if I went with André. And I was still in shock from what had happened. Honestly, I didn't think of anything until I was in the car. Then I had enough sense to demand that André bring me here."

"Which explains what Marcy was saying about a

strange man driving you here and her hearing an argument before you came into the house.''

"Yeah," Sarah replied. "André didn't want to leave me. I didn't mean to hurt him, but he had to understand I didn't love him and wasn't taking the job he offered. I think maybe he realized that I had become his courage to face his father. It was a step he needed to take to finally grow up. But it wasn't love. When it came out that Drydan had just called Justin, I don't think he believed me." She shrugged.

"Oh, Sarah, honey." He reached out and touched her shoulder, then drew back his hand. "Go to Justin. Explain. I know he loves you."

"How? How do you know?"

Bill looked her straight in the eye. "He told me. I don't think he'd honestly care about your infertility. If nothing else, think what you're doing to Mickie in all this."

Sarah knew she looked stricken, but that was one of the reasons she hadn't been able to sleep. "I didn't even get to say goodbye to her."

"Oh, Sarah." Bill sighed. Then he stood and grabbed her by the hand. "Come on. Whether you want to or not, we're going over there."

"I can't. Bill, you don't understand. I don't think he wants me over there."

Bill wouldn't take no for an answer. He pulled her toward the door until she reluctantly followed. "I'll make you a deal. If he gives you any problems, I beat him to a pulp for you."

Sarah laughed, though not out of amusement but

excess nervous energy. "I just don't know...." She hesitated. "I don't want to make things worse."

"Bill! Bill!"

Marcy's frantic voice reached them. Bill threw open the door and Sarah saw Marcy running up the stairs, which were now covered with snow.

Bill immediately released Sarah and ran to Marcy. "What is it, sweetheart? The baby?" His hand went to her abdomen.

"No. Justin called. It's Mickie. She's missing."

Justin paced his house, frantic for any word. Where was she? Where had Mickie gone? She'd been away three hours now.

He'd tucked her in, then come downstairs to work. At one point he'd gone out back to stand in the fresh snow, thinking of all that had happened since Sarah had left, remembering her wish for snow on Christmas so she and Mickie could build a snowman.

He and Mickie were both miserable. They both wanted her back. He'd been praying, trying to decide if her returning would be the best course.

Then he'd gone in and taken a hot shower to warm up. Before getting into bed, he'd gone to check on Mickie. It wasn't until he found her coat and backpack missing that he realized she'd run away.

The pounding on the front door had him racing to it. Bill, Marcy and Sarah stood there.

"Have they found her yet?" Marcy asked, going to him and giving him a hug.

Justin's disappointment was acute. He shook his head. "The police have been out an hour. I've looked all over and haven't been able to spot her. They asked me to stay here in case she calls."

He heard the police officer behind him go back to the phone. They'd left one man behind. He didn't know why. Maybe to keep him there when he finally went crazy and wanted to go back out on the streets and search for his daughter.

"What happened?"

He turned to Bill. "I don't know. I was outside, then I showered. When I went to check on Mickie, she was just gone."

"Any clues?" Bill asked.

Justin finally looked at the last person in the group. He replied to Sarah instead of Bill. "She was miserable this past week. She didn't understand why you'd left."

Sarah appeared tired, as tired as he felt. Deep purple smudges circled her eyes. Guilt etched her face.

"I'm so sorry," she whispered.

He could hear the truth in her voice.

"We should have talked. I should have said goodbye. I should have told you I didn't love André and asked for visitation rights. I don't know what I should have done—"

"Stop it," Justin suddenly whispered, his heart aching. "Come here," he said, and opened his arms.

She ran to him and threw herself at him. He wrapped his arms around her small body and felt her shake with sobs.

"She's so alone, right now," she cried. "Why would she do it?"

"I don't know," he murmured, rocking her. "I just don't know."

He continued to rock her, thinking how right she felt against him. He loved her more than life itself. Why had he ever let her go? Why hadn't he explained that he didn't blame her, that he thought she loved....

"You don't love André?" he questioned, pushing her back. "I don't understand. I thought that's why you left."

Sarah reluctantly released Justin. She looked up and met his gaze. "I left because you told me you thought it was best. Drydan had called you and told... I was going to tell you, Justin. I had the doctor's reports, and even notes to answer questions. They're probably still upstairs on the desk."

"You think I care that you're infertile?" he asked astounded.

She dropped her gaze. "You want more children."

Suddenly angry, he growled, "I *want* you. I *love* you. We can adopt children. My lands, Sarah, didn't you know how much I love you?" Sarah looked up at him and he could see the hope and despair mixed in her eyes.

"No," she whispered. "I didn't."

He jerked her back against him and held on tight, his whole body shaking at the revelation. "Sarah, I asked you if you could love me. What did you think I meant? I want you in my life forever.

"Infertility doesn't matter. If you were blind or crippled it wouldn't matter. Don't you understand, it's you I love.

"Only you.

"Your brightness, your tender spirit, your kindness, thoughtfulness. Just you. All I wanted was your love. Anything else can be overcome. But when I thought you were only considering me because I had given you a job—"

"What?" she asked, shocked. "You thought...how could you?" she asked.

He saw the spark of anger in her eyes and his anger melted.

"I love you for who you are. But you wanted kids. You'd mentioned it and I didn't know if you could accept me after Amy—"

"Whoa, right there," he warned. "The past is the past. Amy was put to rest. I won't ever compare you with her. As I said I want only you."

"You're all I want, too," she said, and went back into his arms. "But, Mickie..."

"Yeah," he said, when she trailed off. "I should have called you and asked you to come over. But I was too proud. I didn't want you to see me like that. I was hurting too much...." He sighed, a defeated sound in a room that should have had only merriment.

Then Sarah's hand cautiously stroked his back, tentatively, as she tried to relieve the hurt and pain he was experiencing.

"Don't blame yourself. We were both wrong. Now all we can do is pray that Mickie is found quickly."

Bill heard that and came forward. Taking their hands, he and Marcy began to pray, asking God to protect her and guide the police to her.

When the door opened, Sarah was the first to see

the bundle in the police officer's arms. She cried out, covering her mouth in joy.

Justin looked up, saw the brown head sticking up out of a blanket and dropped Sarah's and Bill's hands. "Mickie?" he asked, scared to find out if she was hurt. Then it didn't matter. He shot across the room and was reaching out for his daughter. "Mickie, honey?"

Her head popped out of the blanket. Tears covered her face. "I'm sorry, Daddy, but I had to get her."

"Who, honey?" he asked, rubbing her legs and arms, chafing warmth into her. "Where'd you find her?"

"About two miles from here, Mr. Warner," the officer said.

"I had to find Aunt Sarah."

Justin stared at his daughter. His knees were knocking in relief. "You were going to walk to Bill's?"

Mickie shrugged.

"I told you never, ever to try that, honey. You scared us all to death."

The tears started again and Justin immediately felt awful for chastising her. He gathered her close and turned toward Sarah, his only purpose to get her to the woman she had been seeking. Mickie's next words stopped him.

"You don't understand. You said you loved her. And you told me if it was a real emergency I didn't have to wait for a grown-up. I could walk someplace myself."

He started to explain he'd meant to find a teacher or policeman to help her, but she wasn't done.

"I asked Santa for a mommy. I prayed and told

Jesus to send just the right one. Well, Aunt Sarah was just right. You did say you loved her, Daddy. But you see, it's Christmas Eve, and I couldn't find my letter to put on the tree and I was afraid Santa would forget to bring her. I just had to find her.''

Justin couldn't help it; he started crying. He wasn't sure if it was relief or joy.

"Don't cry, Daddy," she whispered. "There's a police officer here and he'll see you."

That caused him to chuckle as tears streamed down his face. Justin continued across the room to where Sarah was crying, too. Halfway there, Mickie saw Sarah.

"You're here!" she cried out, and wiggled from her daddy's grasp. "He found my letter!" She ran over to Sarah and threw her arms around her. "Did Santa find you?" she asked.

"Not exactly," Sarah said, bending down and pulling the small child into her embrace. Mickie locked her arms around her neck, then she pushed back. "But how'd you know to come?" she asked, puzzled.

Sarah looked up at Justin. "Your daddy called me."

Mickie looked up at her daddy. "Does this mean you married her now? I know you said she had to move out until you could get married, but I want her back for good."

Justin turned to Sarah. His heart ached with the love he felt for these two. The officer standing near the door, Bill and Marcy near the stairs—their stares didn't matter. All that mattered was the two people he loved most on the face of this Earth, who stood before him. He smiled at his daughter.

"Well, pumpkin," he drawled, "I don't know. You see, Aunt Sarah has to agree to that. Now, if she will, I know a judge or two who might be romantically inclined and might marry us tonight so Sarah will never have to leave this house again. What do you think about that?"

Mickie jumped up and down and turned hopeful eyes on her aunt Sarah. "Oh, please, Aunt Sarah. Will you marry us? I promise to be real good and not ask for chocolate coconut cake again."

"She can't bake that, sweetheart," Justin said, enjoying the look on Sarah's face.

"I won't even ask for too many peanut butter-and-jelly sandwiches," Mickie said, though reluctantly. Then, turning wide eyes on Sarah, she said, "We love you, Aunt Sarah, and want you here." She fidgeted, as if she were afraid of Sarah's answer.

Fresh tears streaked down Sarah's face and she leaned down and hugged Mickie. "And I love you, too. I'll be glad to marry you—and your daddy. Do you think I should tell him?"

Justin's heart tripped over. "I think he heard you," he said, and walked forward. "How about giving me a kiss to seal that?"

Sarah looked up from Mickie, her cheeks suddenly flushing. Her eyes sparkled with love. Slowly, Sarah stood and walked forward. Shyly, she held out her hand. Justin took it, then pulled her into his arms, but he hesitated as he stared at her beautiful face.

"Come on!" Bill called out. Marcy laughed and urged him on, as well.

"An audience," he murmured. Then, not letting

that stop him, he shifted her and bent her back over his arm. "Your acceptance kiss," he said softly before taking her lips.

The kiss left Sarah weak and breathless, supported only by his arms. When she opened her eyes, Mickie was clapping.

"Do it again, Daddy. Do it again."

Justin was short of breath, but looking very smug, Sarah noticed. He smiled and shook his head. "I think I'll save the next one for after we say 'I do.'"

Sarah blushed, then she said tenderly, stroking his face. "I love you, Justin. You're the best Christmas present I've ever received."

Justin pushed her hair behind her ear and nodded. "Let's go find the judge."

Mickie ran up and grabbed her daddy around the legs. He picked her up and started toward the door.

"You know what, Daddy?" she asked.

"What's that, pumpkin?" he said.

"This is gonna be the best Christmas ever."

Looking over at Sarah, he said, "I couldn't agree more."

* * * * *

Dear Reader,

I love kids. And I'm very blessed to have two wonderful, loving children as well as a loving husband. However, not everyone is that lucky. Some people have children but have lost their spouse. Others are married but are unable to have children. This story is about two such people: a woman who comes face-to-face with the possibility of never having children, and a man who has found himself alone, doing his best to raise his daughter.

But with God, all things are possible. In my story, God brings two hurting people together to allow their healing and love to blossom. I'm an eternal optimist and believe there is no situation that God can't turn around for good. With His love leading us, He can give us joy and the true desires of our hearts if we only stop and listen to His voice. I hope you have enjoyed Sarah and Justin's story, as together they discovered God's plan for their lives—along with a little help from Justin's rambunctious daughter, Mickie. I'd love to hear from you, too. Write to me c/o Steeple Hill Books, 233 Broadway, Suite 1001, New York, NY 10279.

Cheryl Wolverton